THE END AND E

'Mysterious, poetic, earthy and profound, *The —
Before It* is a true delight, unlike anything I've ever read.'
Ayelet Waldman

'Moving, profound and deeply layered…A triumphant melding
of time and place, grief and love, and above all, the strength
of the human spirit to counter tragedy with hope and endure.'
*Books+Publishing*

'A lyrical story about the inevitability of events, of chance moments,
of threads slowly woven together…The reward is a love story and a
bit of magic…Kruckemeyer will crush your cynicism with a velvet
glove. The novel's climax might break your heart but you will
be thankful for the reminder of the importance of life's everyday
miracles…A celebration of the natural world, a wonderful argument
against capitalism and a welcome antidote to dark times.'
*Saturday Paper*

'Beguiling…A parable of survival that attests to the value of resilient
social bonds. We need writers who can anatomise the forces that
are tearing our world apart—and we have them in abundance.
Kruckemeyer has taken on a different task: envisioning what is
required of us to build a world in which we can thrive.'
*Guardian*

'Beautifully demonstrates how stories can connect and shape
lives, transcending generations and geographical boundaries…
Masterful storytelling and rich character development create
an immersive reading experience that lingers in the mind
even after the story concludes.'
Readings

'Unputdownable…uplifting…quietly devastating.'
*ANZ LitLovers*

Finegan Kruckemeyer was born in Ireland and grew up in Adelaide. He is an award-winning playwright whose works have been performed on six continents and in eight languages. *The End and Everything Before It* is his first novel.

# THE END
## AND
# EVERYTHING
## BEFORE
## IT

FINEGAN KRUCKEMEYER

TEXT PUBLISHING MELBOURNE AUSTRALIA

The Text Publishing Company acknowledges the Traditional Owners of the country on which we work, the Wurundjeri people of the Kulin Nation, and pays respect to their Elders past and present.

textpublishing.com.au

The Text Publishing Company
Wurundjeri Country, Level 6, Royal Bank Chambers, 287 Collins Street, Melbourne Victoria 3000 Australia

Published in Australia and New Zealand by The Text Publishing Company, 2024
Reprinted 2024

Cover design by W. H. Chong
Cover images from iStock
Page design by Imogen Stubbs
Typeset by J&M Typesetting

Printed and bound in Australia by Griffin Press, a member of the Opus Group. The Opus Group is ISO/NZS 14001:2004 Environmental Management System certified.

ISBN: 9781922790736 (paperback)
ISBN: 9781922791795 (ebook)

A catalogue record for this book is available from the National Library of Australia.

The paper this book is printed on is certified against the Forest Stewardship Council® Standards. Griffin Press, a member of the Opus Group, holds chain of custody certification SCS-COC-001185. FSC® promotes environmentally responsible, socially beneficial and economically viable management of the world's forests.

*For Es, who conquered a year*
*For Moe, who walked me through it*

*The bad news is you're falling through the air, nothing to hang on to, no parachute. The good news is there's no ground.*

Chögyam Trungpa

## PART ONE

# EBBING

# 1

## Emma the Greek

In the two weeks my family and I are lost at sea, we float a great distance.

They call me Emma the Greek but I am not Greek. I am olive-skinned, though, and on our wintery land this is odd enough for a nickname. My mama was a slut and had me with a travelling sailor. Says my papa. He does not know if the sailor was Greek—he does not even know if this is true—but since forever Emma the Greek is my name.

I cannot ask Mama the truth, because the sea carries no messages to the ones who lie at its bottom. Or even if it does, it brings no replies back to the surface.

In the two weeks we are lost at sea, we share the little food we saved from the trawler before it sank. We threw tin cans in the lifeboat quickly, and my little brother said, 'Not those ones, Emma the Greek!'

'Don't talk bullshit, Paddy!' roared Papa. 'Food is food. Hurry up or I leave you.'

Papa is unforgiving and a taskmaster. But he saved us from Mama's ocean and for this I thank him. Thank you, Papa.

On the twelfth day, my big brother Ulli says, 'One of us will not survive.'

And this is the biggest surprise, as Ulli has not said a single word for six years. The doctor said a black hole grew in his brain, and the black hole sucked up all the words he'd ever learnt in the fourteen years before, and then he had no more words. But I thought another thing—I thought, maybe this was Ulli waiting for the right words.

On the last day, snow sits on the water, and we do not have to fear the small hole in the boat because ice forms across it and seals it—amazing. But Papa says, 'This is the coldest night, boys and girl. And Emma the Greek does not stop shivering.'

'I am okay, Papa.'

'You shut up now, Emma the Greek. Boys, we take off our jumpers and give them to the girl.'

'No, Papa!' says Paddy.

And Ulli—he says nothing.

But they all three take off their jumpers and put them on me, and I am too tired to argue, and I feel warm for the first time in days. Why do they not make a normal jumper that is four jumpers thick, I think. This would be a great invention.

And then I go to sleep, and as my eyes are closing, I see Papa and Paddy and Ulli in their old shirts, huddled together at the end of the boat. Papa is rubbing his sons' shoulders like a great big bear. He is a very good father.

And later, when we hit the shore, I wake up and I smile at Papa and Ulli and Paddy. And two of them look back at me. But Paddy—he has blue skin and a look that is not for us anymore, but for Mama now. He can talk to Mama now, I understand this. So before we tie the boat and step onto land, we give him to the sea.

Goodbye, Paddy Blue Skin.

∞

Papa got extremely ill three nights ago.

His head was as hot as the stove—honestly, if I put one hand on him and one on the stove, I do not know which would burn first. Well, not honestly, but you know what I mean.

Ulli and I call the doctor, but he is far away and without petrol. He says to make many flannels wet and to sit these on Papa, on his head and his shoulders and his chest. He says he will send antibiotics tomorrow, but tomorrow is a thousand years away when your one and only papa is as hot as a stove.

Papa is so weak he cannot leave the armchair. He coughs over and over and his tongue swells. We feed him water through a straw and take turns sitting there with him, like a good son and a good daughter. We take turns sleeping too.

And you are scared to sleep, because once before when you slept Paddy Blue Skin died. But this is nonsense. I have slept a thousand times since then, and sometimes I wake up to sunshine and sometimes to rain. But never again to death.

I wake now on this morning and Ulli is doing an unusual thing. He has Mama's old scissors and he is cutting off Papa's beard. Papa lies back in the armchair watching Ulli's face and Ulli is immensely focused. And I can see what a great idea this is. Papa is so hot and a beard makes you hotter and now it is going, falling onto his bare chest in great, grey curls.

I have only ever known Papa as a bearded man. But today, right now, he is someone else. He has a chin I have never met and his cheeks are round—I always thought his head was large because of the hair. But his head is large.

'You have no beard,' I tell my papa.

And he and Ulli stop and look at me, my brother and a new man looking at me. And Papa coughs, and gasps for breath, and wipes his hand through the dirty mat of chopped-off hair stuck to his sweaty, large cheeks. And he says, 'You and Ulli are taking the boat out today.'

∞

We stand in the boat together, Ulli and me, Emma the Greek. And I say, 'Your knots in the net are the shittest knots I have seen in a million years. All the fish are swimming right through the big stupid holes and telling their friends you are ridiculous.'

And Ulli says nothing. Which is the great pleasure of ridiculing my brother. He will say not one word back. He throws a mackerel at my head, though, and it gives me a black eye. And if I was a proper girl, like one who can wear make-up and has boyfriends and did not leave school at fourteen to fish with her papa, I would have cried. Instead I spit over the side and say, 'Fuck you.'

Then we fish together all afternoon and until it is dark.

In the night-time, we play cards and drink whisky and talk about Papa. And the way we talk is that I speak and Ulli nods or shakes or flicks me with a card or pours more whisky. Or sometimes he writes on paper.

Neither of us can believe that Papa is not here. This is his boat and he is captain and a hard worker and a taskmaster. And in my nineteen years, he has never missed a work day: always on the land for four days and away for four days, and on the land for four days. And away. And when each of us turned fourteen, we did this with him—four days, and four days, and four days, always. Paddy Blue Skin only did a little time of this, and he sleeps with Mama now, for all the days.

I pick my nose for a bit while Ulli writes. And then he shows me the paper, and it says:

> *This morning, when he was in the doorway as we left, with no beard and the blanket around him like an old woman, I felt like he was younger than us, like we were the parents and he was the kid.*

7

And I say maybe Papa is like Samson, from the Bible, and Ulli has made him weak by cutting his hair. Ulli hits me with an ashtray and I spit whisky in his eyes so he screams (he can still scream). And then we go to bed.

I wake up and it is four in the morning and the waves are rough. Ulli's bunk is empty. I climb onto the deck and there he is. He has gone for a piss off the side and a large wave has come from out of the darkness and knocked him backwards onto the jag. He is lying on the deck and, even though he is on top of it, I can see the jag hook because it is coming out through his chest. Blood is coming out of his mouth and, just as rare, words are coming out of his mouth too.

'I fell onto the jag. It is inside me, Emma the Greek. It is going through me. I can feel my heart pump against the metal—*boom, boom*, like this, just here.'

He stopped and it seemed like the end, but there was more.

'You are the last one I will see, little sister. And you were the last one Paddy Blue Skin saw before he went to Mama. And you were the last one Mama saw before she went to the sea. And maybe Papa too—when you see him, it will be the last thing too. Because you are a terrible magic, Emma the Greek. You carry death with you. You carry it and…*Haaa!* I just felt…my heart…explode…against the metal…It is…
……………'

I roll up my brother in a bedsheet. But before I cover his face, I give him a chance to say something else to me, any last thing that is not about me carrying death.

But Ulli is silent. Ulli is nearly always silent.

I haul him up with all my strength and give him to the ocean.

Then I drink all the whisky, and think about Papa. And the terrible magic I carry with me.

And how to keep him alive.

∞

I have made my choice, and it is to stay on the water forever. Ulli, as well as being an annoying brother and a poor net fixer and now a dead man, was right. I am the last one seen by three of my family—and Papa, if he sees me, will die too. He is sick, he has no beard now, he cannot fish.

And so, I will sail a long time. I will give my papa a long life.

# 2

## Isaac, the Prisoner

When I inherited the land, I had little.

Little to eat, little to live on and little company, little to justify my existence. I could be here or I could not, and little would it matter. Then I inherited the land.

It was a large acreage and the great-uncle Henry who'd died was an unknown figure in my life—a man who went to a war and remained there, laid out on some stretch of cold ground after the others returned home. As a child, I went with my parents to a small graveyard each year and we would sombrely find his name and leave a flower maybe—I can't say for sure.

Over the next years, a slow succession of deaths occurred:

the wife of that great uncle, some cousins—and eventually my parents too, in the depths of a season when rains are heavy and wagons are given to taking corners badly and sliding off country roads into rickety barns, which then collapse and flatten all beneath them.

At the same time—as branches of my family tree were being pruned by time and fate—I experienced a contraction of my own, of livelihood and love and liberty.

First a job at a bank ceased to be, for no reason I can provide. The resulting lack of funds led to domestic stress, I think that's the polite term, and not long after that I said goodbye to a wife I loved. I got sad then, and that sadness congealed into an anger aimed at all—my temper grew ever shorter, my voice ever louder.

Until that particular night when a passing policeman ordered me be quiet. And I ordered him to stop ordering me. Our echoed roars shifted into the physical then, and—what, really, is there to say?—a man's body passed through a window. A shard of glass found an artery, blood ran into the gutter of that wholly unimportant street, and I was suddenly a member of our country's fine prison system. So it goes.

Fourteen years I spent behind high walls, on a high hill, dividing my time between tending a small garden, reading what few books were imprisoned with us, and fending off the attacks of the more volatile prisoners. The garden suffered in the heat, the books became too familiar, the brutes got their release one at a time, and life took on a pattern I understood.

And then came the singular day: my name is called, Great Uncle Henry's death is announced, the inherited land is presented, and the prison director (good man he is) deems me rehabilitated and free to go.

The gates open—I walk.

∞

The chair I sit in at the lawyer's office is narrow and squeaky but the desk is firm and true and across it we discuss how things might best play out. He will give me ten pound for the land, he tells me. And this price is more than fair, he tells me. And my choices are few so of course I cannot say no, he tells me.

And I tell him, with a shake of my head, no.

He squeaks.

I am firm.

I leave.

For days I roam my ten-pound piece of land without map or compass. One boundary is the sea, and there is an estuary and a river which snakes from far inland. Beside that river, a long patient stretch of soil, full of promise. And behind this arable pasture, a forest dense and secretive. In its canopy, a million birds dart and tumble, build nests and tend their young.

On the forest's other side (where I can lay no claim) a hill rises, bare and brutish, the trees of its slopes callously razed so no cover might hide a fleeing prisoner. A hill which at its top holds a prison. Which in its recent history held me.

I walk, feeling the earth beneath my feet, feeling my liberty in the verdant ground and the woods that teem with life. I climb trees and find nests and walk fence lines, unable to fathom that all held within them is mine—that the world it has forgiven me, or forgotten me, I can't be sure which.

I think back over a life gone wayward. And I think forward, imagining what men better than I might do next. And I decide.

I plant crops in great furrows carved by an ox, with me plodding behind and steering the plough. Into these furrows I throw seed, and then irrigate the earth and watch the water flow upon slowly darkening soil. I ask the sun to shine, and shine it does.

I sell some outer reaches of my property and with this money I buy animals and hire a local man to tend them. I never meet him though—only seal the deal with a letter sent, a fee offered. And he sets to work with the quiet resolve of a farming man.

I walk into my forest and fell a number of broad-trunked trees, careful to leave the canopy intact. I buy a small hand-mill, and read books about such things, and cut the wood into great lengths. I read more books and I shape those lengths, fashioning the wood into tables many metres long, and long benches that run either side. I clear the undergrowth around them to form a dining room that knows no walls.

This business has taken me months, novice that I am. I

return to the fields of furrowed land, the enclosures of pig and cow and hen, and find all just as it should be—the crops are tall and proud, the animals fat and docile, content to chew grass and lie in shade, their eyelids heavy.

I take in the picture, then read more books and learn more skills and buy more tools. I harvest the grain and vegetables, slaughter the animals. Bread is baked, salads made, and a giant bed of hot coals is laid out on the clearing's floor. Then every pig and cow and chicken is placed on its own spit and set above the heat, rotating slowly.

The aroma seeps into the air and passes over the countryside. It floats into every window of every home (even finding its way to the prison where for so long little entered, little left). Those living nearby have been sent letters of invitation and asked to spread the word.

That evening I go to my clearing in the forest, and I wait.

I have laid a thousand forks and knives, a thousand plates. I wait at a greeting place and when the first arrive—a family of four with flame-red hair—and the father extends his hand to me, I realise I have not spoken a word for fourteen years, and that last word was *Guilty*. And the ones before it were slurred and violent. I do not know if I can speak anymore.

But I open my mouth and manage something simple. The woman kisses me on each cheek, as is the custom in the region, and the children nod their heads. First it is awkward between us, but then across the fields I see the tide coming in, as every person (from every farm and house and wretched lean-to in the foothills) comes to shake my hand and kiss my cheeks.

They do not know the man they meet, but they smell the food and see the benches empty and waiting. And they know what to do. They sit. They spread napkins over gingham skirts and work-worn trousers. They talk among themselves, they laugh. And I savour that laughter, those conversations. I feel the clearing fill with words. I feel the canopy above hold those words in.

Soon the sun sets and the moon rises, and I send matches down the tables so a thousand candles can be lit, and a thousand flames dance. As I pass a box to one woman—young, bonneted—my hand lingers, or hers does, I suspect neither of us knows which. She nods. I smile. Our hands separate. It is only a moment, but it is a moment.

When everyone has found their place, the meat is cut, the salads passed, the plates filled. Then all eyes turn to me. They are not eyes of absolution or forgiveness, because these people do not know my past. They are eyes of neighbours, pure and simple, with looks that speak of reciprocity and a long day's work now done. They wait.

I raise a glass and say, with little fanfare: 'Thank you for visiting, new friends. I look forward to the day you are old ones.'

And they nod, as though these words are correct.

Then, as the warm wind moves the leaves above, we take up knives and forks.

We share a happy smile.

And we feast.

# 3

## Isaac's Vision

The feast is a great success. Not because I am the best host, or the food is the best food (though I hold a nice enough conversation, and the meat served could not be more succulent). But because of the parts that make the whole.

The forest canopy is an umbrella rich with every green. The moonlight filtering through it, a gentle constant. The fire coals warm us. The tables are busy thoroughfares along which the things of life pass back and forth—salad bowls, misplaced forks, conversation, bottles of ale. And laughter. Laughter ringing off glasses, clattering onto plates, making eyes shine, cheeks crease. I sit in the laughter, happy to have set the table that holds it.

The bonneted woman I do not see again. As the feast dwindles and the fires die down, I imagine finding her, laughing with her. Sitting side by side on a bench and talking of lives before. Talking, if all went well, of lives to come. One conversation among a hundred, one quiet chat heard above every other voice. But though I scan the crowd—pass my eyes up and down the length of every table—I do not find her.

As the night wears on, bottles empty, jokes grow coarser, children sleepier (curled on mothers' laps or poking at the glowing coals with gnarled sticks). Until eventually I sit with thirty or so of the farming men and women, and we make plans.

They like my quiet way. I don't mention it is only half a lifetime old, learned in a prison where quiet days were safe and loud ones dangerous. That before those years I was a man forged by a city, inheriting its volume, its insatiable thirst. I don't mention this and they don't ask—a deal done in its not-doing.

And, besides me, they like my land. The river mouth full of hearty, gullible fish. The fields where animals grazed and fattened and were felled. This forest in which we now sit, with its million birds roosting above us. And beyond, the rise towards the hill with its prison I know from inside and out. Where the woods end, there my boundary lies—and this is right, as I am a man for owning land and rivers and possibility. Not punishment, not penance.

Ale swapped for whisky, cigarettes rolled, we talk until

sun-up about what this land is to be—what I might enjoy and what they might need.

Which is a town.

The farmers own farms, a plot per family. Some large, some small. And in their fields they grow their crops and graze their stock, in their farmhouses they live. But the places for coming together—the market square where reaped harvests may be sold, the schoolhouse, the tavern, the church—those are all a long cart ride away. You must plan for those things, must bundle your wares, load up your children and travel. And then, yes, you return richer, or poorer, or cleverer or sadder or surer, but always with a long journey taken.

The farms sit shoulder to shoulder, leaning on one another with stone-piled walls between them. And in the past no family has wished to sacrifice its land for a town—and this is right. The land is theirs. The industry and profit and weight of time-hewn honour is theirs. But my plot—my estuary, river, pastures, woods—these are not bogged down in obligation, in history. Except of a bad kind.

The farmers wait hours to admit it, embarrassed by what they regret to say and not wishing to sully this good man before them with stories of the bad blood in his veins. My great-uncle—who went to war and died at war and left this land behind him—was not a good man.

Steeped in money and living in a big house in a faraway place, he'd been many things, few of them scrupulous, all of them profitable. The man had gambled and won as poor men tumbled. His coffers grew, his morals fled, he became richer—and all the worse for it.

And then a war, which he tried of course to buy his way out of. But the politician he beseeched was, as fate would have it, the brother of a broken man now destitute, every coin lost in one of my great-uncle's promises. And so, money bedamned, to Russia he went. Into a volley he walked. On a tundra he fell. Rich and dead is still dead.

'When we heard he'd left the land to you, we figured you must be mean too,' admits Ed O'Brian through his thick beard.

'Only happy it ain't so,' says Ruth Mulholland.

'Happy that,' nod a couple of others.

And the happiness is felt all round. A drink is passed to me, and the drink is a handshake, just in another form.

'I believe...' I say, and they lean in a little to hear my belief. 'I never could make sense of why all this fell my way? He had others closer, ones who shared his name, shared his home who should have received it. But I believe that's the exact point. Him being not a kindly man, like you say, it stands to reason he finished with an unkind act. Maybe a desire to put some salt in their wounds—and maybe some spice in mine. Maybe a plan to set me on a path of doing no good, reaping what I didn't sow and deciding I can chart a course through a life that way. Turn me ruthless like him maybe. 'Cept the thing is...'

I draw a breath here, and it pulls the leaning folk in with it.

'I've been ruthless already. I didn't just come from no place. I came from that place.'

I look up towards the hill, but can't look back—not at one of them, not in the face. Until I do—and what I see is a surprise. Smiling eyes, happy mouths.

'We know,' says one, and he shrugs. 'Every one of us has been inside at one time. We know that place.'

And they nod, and watch the fire, giving me a moment. And when after a time I take a swig and pass the drink along, then (like condensation on the bottle offered) that story is gone, and it doesn't need ever to be told again.

'This ain't no swindle neither,' says Seb Claybourne. 'If a farmer's what you mean to be, then go be it and we'll teach you the things you mightn't know yet. All we're saying is a township seems more of a—what d'ya call it? A win–win. You give the nod and we all help build a main street through those paddocks there. Down at the coast, a jetty heading off the end of that street and out to sea. Then the river side of the street we leave be, and the not-river side we'll build a hardware store and a food store and a small church and a tavern for old Lukey to go swimmin' in.'

'Go fuck yerself,' mutters Luke Turner, and everyone laughs, him too.

'And then you become a man who rents buildings,' continues Claybourne. 'Which is a hell of a lot easier thing to learn than farming if I'm honest.'

'And if you want a title,' offers a short man they call Gnome, 'well it can be Mayor or whatever else you might fancy on.'

'Oh, I wouldn't need a title,' I say quietly. And this answer makes everyone sit back on their benches and know their proposition was right.

Then slowly, one by one, they go their separate ways, each taking up a travelling bottle, giving a small wave and walking back over one hill or another, the land now purple in the near-dawn light, the first birds daring us to ask the time with their stirrings.

Until only I remain. A man filling just one seat of many seats. The dishes cleaned and stacked hours before by busy, practical hands. The coals whispering last breaths. The flames gone. The food gone. Leaves remaining. Air remaining. Time remaining.

*Climb off this bench now, old man, and go lie down in the dirt.*

*Lie on your back. Feel your knots loosen. Stare up at the trees. See the trees stare down. Breathe. Owe nothing. Need nothing. Breathe. Sleep.*

# 4

## Nella Sands, the Seer

She was not meant for children. One doctor after another had said it, looming over her as she lay uncomfortable on a narrow bed in the cold hospital on the bare hill, knees pointing to the ceiling but collapsing in on each other in an embarrassed hillock of their own. The doctor would mutter something, then rise and remove gloves and light a cigarette.

'We'll talk further outside,' he'd say, and wander off.

The woman, who was Nella Sands, would be left, in those sterile moments, to drag her knickers up defeated legs and stare off down the barren slope through a window that no longer needed bars but had forgotten to tell itself this. The hospital remembered all too well the prison it had been a hundred years ago. Nowadays it was tasked with saving lives, yes, but all it would agree to was extra time, not salvation. Up here, your life might stretch on a little longer. But being here would not make you better. This hilltop was too hard for that.

Only beyond the slope—down there where the forest began, where the birds flew, the town lay, the sea lapped the shore—only there could a true heartbeat be found.

Nella would nod a self-conscious thank you to the nurse avoiding her eye, take her handbag, and go to the small room where doctor and husband would sit either side of a desk and talk mournfully about her womb, as she listened politely on a small chair nearby.

∞

She was not meant for children—one doctor after another had said it—so her husband left.

He walked to the letterbox at the end of the garden in the dunes, turned and stared. She waved pleasantly from the window. Then he opened the rusted-hinge gate and was gone.

Soon he was living with a woman who smoked a pipe and hung torn dresses from the tree in front of her house to scare the crows away.

Nella Sands was a practical one, though, and she went and knocked on the door of her husband's new home.

He answered and shook his head pityingly. 'I'm here now. Don't make things any harder.'

Nella leant sideways, dodging his words and in the same action looking over his shoulder and down the corridor. 'Lucy. Lucy Sykes—I see you back there in the kitchen, standing over those potatoes. I didn't come for trouble. I came for trade.'

She waited patiently on the porch while her once-husband whispered with his now-woman, and finally Lucy came—though she carried a skillet, swinging it casually like it was just a cooking thing and not a weapon should claws come out.

'You can put down the pan, girl, or keep it in your hand, it doesn't matter to me. You have him now and I offer equal parts congratulation and condolence—he's a good kisser, but a weak one for lifting things. Anyway, love talk doesn't pass well between the once-had and the now-has, so I'll get to business.

'You've been single six years and I imagine your house is set up in that fashion. Only now there's two of you and you'll be needing twice the bed at night and an extra chair come breakfast time. So here's my offer—trade me your single things (your one chair, your narrow bed, your fork, spoon, knife) and in return I'll hand over my doubles fit for a man and a woman. And to balance out the lopsidedness of that transaction, give me those dresses hanging in the tree there.'

It was a good deal, no denying, so the transaction was made, and the furniture and bits and bobs were set up in their new homes (just Nella's long wooden table stayed put, too large a thing to fit through the door). Which only left the collection of the dresses, and to the man between the two, this job went. He climbed the tree begrudgingly, dropped garments down, then slipped and fell on his way back to earth.

The leg was broken in two places and a long stretch of bedrest followed. The man pined during these days for that pipe-smoking woman to warm the place beside him, but without the dresses flapping in the tree she was left all day long to fend off the crows, who would strip her garden bare of fruit and who spared her no time for cuddling.

The man, abandoned so, lay in that bed, which was double the size, yes, but half-filled all the same. And he smelled the once-woman on the sheets, he felt the indent formed by her after all those years of lying beside him. And he knew this now-woman could never fill it. Realising wrongs committed, he hobbled to the letterbox which held no mail, past the trees that bore no fruit, and beyond the woman whose smoking cough hacked at the cool air. And again, he closed a gate. Again he walked.

Nella acknowledged him as he shambled over the dunes, opened the creaking gate, limped through the garden, up the porch steps and to her door, once his.

Again he said it. 'I'm here now. Don't make things any harder.'

And without a word she let him in, and showed him what his once-house had become. A narrow bed made for one, books piled around it that only she liked reading. Here a chair that had no partner, there on the stove a kettle boiled with water just enough for a single cup of tea.

'And so you see,' she said to him. 'It isn't a matter of choice no more. You just don't fit.'

And politely she waited with screen door held open as he guppy-fished his mouth which was devoid of words, and turned his head in each direction, looking for something that might be his. But sometimes there's no denying the shifting state of things, and the ripples in the pond, and the general fact that mistakes are mistakes, and a broken shin can't change them. And he hobbled out as he had hobbled in, and walked a garden path again, and passed a letterbox again, and stood beside a bin that held a pile of discarded frocks, their purpose served. And he held a gate again, unsure.

Nella heard the kettle whistle and walked away to answer it, not waiting to see which way her rusty hinges swung.

∞

She was not made for children—one doctor after another had said it—so she busied herself with other things. She had long since forgotten the man, closed her ears to the gossip, and settled into her solitary life, single-bedded and untroubled. Her once-husband, she heard, had cut down the tree in Lucy Sykes' front yard. Then he and she had settled on the porch, in matching chairs, and watched over the seasons as the crows ate what they wished. They said little, this dull-spirited pair, and in that silence found a peace that surprised all.

Nella gave herself to small rituals, well rationed. At dawn she rose and walked her garden in the dunes, checking her plants. The kettle's whistle brought her in, and she held the cup in two curved hands, the tea sipped until it was gulping temperature, then gulped.

The townsfolk took her quiet way to be wisdom, and they came to visit in their ones and twos and threes. Nella, well possessed of practicality, knew she needed food and firewood, so she took to leaving a coin jar inside the front door. This way any man or woman could wander in (knocking a formality soon forgotten) and vent their problems to Nella, and have those same words spoken back, in a slightly shuffled order that imbued them with good sense. Relieved, they would depart unburdened and, on noticing the jar (or the woman's polite cough if not the jar), pat their pockets, find a coin and drop it in.

Sometimes someone would stumble in so laden with guilt or shock or despair or love that they couldn't conjure words. And Nella Sands would lead them to the kitchen and sit them at her worn old table, and stare at them from the doorway with arms crossed. Or she would take them to the garden and walk with them a lap of it, studying her plants but studying also her company and what species their eyes fell on first. Or she would lie them on her single bed and ruminate upon their horizontal form. And eventually she would have it.

> *It is your daughter. You fear for her heart in the hands of this man she loves.*
> *It is your husband—you feel an echoing gulf as you face each other at dinner.*

*It is your dog—it does not run to you when entering the*
*kitchen anymore.*
*It is the weather.*
*It is a man you owe money who waits outside your*
*house with chin raised high.*
*It is the rain.*
*It is the ghost of your grandmother, who watches as you*
*lie in bed each night.*

And every time her words were just the thing. And she
would coax the story from them, and watch it form, and treat
it in a way that soothed the teller. And then cough politely,
receive her pennies, and send them out the door.

Eventually she would ask that a visitor say nothing, and
simply sit, or stand, or lie, or garden-walk, until she found the
root of their pain. Nella Sands was a gardener of the human
condition, and she could weed the worry from you.

# 5

## The Man on the Bicycle

She was not meant for children—one doctor after another had said it—but none from that profession had cared to tell the man who entered town.

For a long time Nella Sands had been divining the inner workings of her fellow townsfolk, and it could be said her gift had worked its wonders. Men who once came home filled with anger, filled so full it sloshed over the sides and caused chairs to bust and kids to cling to mother-legs, now entered sated and made quarrel with no one. Women long beset by fidgety anxiety—with nails bitten low, and cheeks gaunt, and shaky desperation in their eyes—now glided down the footpaths of the town serenely. Skittish children had been calmed, and so their parents breathed calmer also. The heart of the town beat a little slower, and it was Nella Sands who made it so.

Nella liked their esteem, if her humble way would let it be known. Her penny jar was mostly full, most of the time, and an observant passer-by might note new shingles on her porch roof, and the planting of rare and hard-to-chance-upon species in her garden soil, a small oasis there beside the sea.

She enjoyed also this knowing of things, for it was a true and real gift. She felt herself a kindred spirit to the thin-moustachioed clock-mender who kept a store on the main street—she, like he, understood that process of opening up a thing, studying its many tiny parts and (in reading how the cogs conjoined) coming to know the larger form and why it ran the way it did.

But her belly held nothing, and this thought sat heavy in her heart. Alas, for bellies to grow, one requires a dance that single beds don't readily accommodate and a person with whom to partner. So it only stood to reason that sooner or later he would come.

He arrived as all slept on a Sunday night—on a bicycle laden with wicker crates, and hidden beneath a tilted hat, smelling of a sipping liquor swigged, if strength of stench was any guessing. As he rode through the town he sang a truly beautiful song, and the sleeping ones in beds sighed happy as it climbed inside their dreams.

The riding got slower and eventually inertia had its way. The bicycle tipped and settled its passenger in the gutter. A wise man would have laughed then at the silliness of such a thing—the man laughed.

He climbed out from beneath his bike, then fixed his hat—which had landed straight—back to its sloping angle and staggered to an alleyway. 'Stay,' he told the bicycle, then laughed, then hiccupped, then slid down the wall as tiredness placed a caring hand upon his shoulder and bade him go to ground.

Collapsed in the shadows, he said a silent prayer of thanks (that was to no single god, but rather all of them at once) for getting him through another day and, smiling at the stars, he slept.

∞

He was not meant for children—one time after another he had said it. But still the thought came to him often, in his dreams.

∞

The sunlight was a cruel thing as it cut across the man's eyelids. Muttering some words that were for no god to be hearing, he lifted himself and glanced down the alley. There stood his bicycle, no longer in the gutter but now leant carefully against a lamppost. And from this simple repositioning the man understood that this was a town that gave itself to the righting of fallen things, and knew he would linger here a while.

The town's main business relied on an orchard valley and a river—the fruit picked in one would be floated down the other in big heavy boats that didn't care if it was today or a hundred years ago. They were captained by old men with curved spines, and crewed by the quiet ones who'd left school early. You looked any one of them in the eye in silence, and he'd hold your gaze forever. But say a word and he'd stare out along the river like you'd never been there at all.

As he walked down Main Street that first time, the man noticed the coloured shopfronts and the big pair of scissors hanging outside the hairdresser and Rhoda in her wheelchair in front of her mum's bar and the bridge and the trees and the season here he was sure was different from the one two miles back. The river was a sloth that day and the boats did not need tying. The fruit was ripening on the trees, and schoolboys sat beneath the branches, teaching each other swear words.

The man sat in a park, on a bench, for some hours, taking it all in. And then—a new day's thirst dawning—he cut across to the bar. He nodded to the girl in the chair, walked in the door, pulled out a stool and drank a beer the name of which was new to him.

Barbara asked him how he was, and he said, 'Good.' And then she asked if he was passing through, and again it was short. 'Yes ma'am,' and a nod to round it off. But already it was there: the hint of something far-reaching stretching out from this nothing moment. Like maybe one day again he'd sit and Barbara would ask how he was—only it'd be twenty years later and his hair would be a different colour and he would be calmer and someone would be sitting beside him.

The man finished his drink, thanked Barbara, and went out to the porch and the autumn sun. The girl in the wheelchair watched him walk down the steps and back to his bicycle. And he would have got on it too—he would have ridden away and called that that and this this. But the river's slothfulness was hypnotic in that moment. The boats moored, their day's work done, and their crews silent on deck, drinking beer and watching the sky.

And in that second, Arthur drove past in his truck, which held a piano in need of fixing. And to a local this was common as day—but to a wandering man, an unanchored man, a piano's a bit of a magical thing to see being driven down the street. And then you add to that the great many birds perched on the roof ridge across the way. And the sound of Ivy Keene's harp wafting out of her attic room. And Rhoda balancing there on the back wheels of her chair like it was nothing at all. And the temperature that's just right for wiping the hair off your neck, and the bridge to the right, and the memory of that beer just downed, and a day moon visible above, and a kid under a tree laughing somewhere nearby, having just heard the rudest word there is, and the red leaves falling, and a cat sitting on a windowsill.

And whatever your thinking, some moments have a weight to them, enough that they make a man with only a bike and some baskets to his name suddenly think of a thing he wasn't expecting, a thing that might get thought about only in dreams. That's all can be said, really—that it was one of those moments.

And it's true to say it was felt by every single person in town. Because they all came out onto their porches, or stood up on their decks, or stepped out of their wheelchairs.

And, as one, they tipped their hats.

∞

Nella heard hinges swinging, and she wiped her hands on a dishcloth, and placed the needle down on a record that had warped a little, summer having burned sharp as it did. She stood and waited for the screen door to open, hands on hips and eyes drawn to that warped record as it went round and round, the stylus like a bicycle rolling up and down its pitch-black hills.

The way the man entered was calamitous and strange. He wiped his feet on the mat, then opened the screen door so it hit against his toes—as though his boots and that door's arc overlapping was a fact strange to him. He stepped back then, but now found himself too far away to reach the handle. He laughed—to himself, to the door—then stepped aside, opened the screen and smiled, triumphant.

Nella immediately liked this man who would think the opening of a door something worth celebrating. He seemed like one who counted days by their small successes, not their tragedies. What a thing that was.

The man impressed her a second time then, by knocking.

And when she walked to the door, the man smiled. And when he smiled, so did she.

He shifted his feet, embarrassed, upending the money jar and sending coins rolling across the porch and through the gaps between the boards. Both watched this dance of disappearing wealth, a thousand coins falling down to earth. And both watched the other not scrambling, as if agreeing they were not worth lying on one's belly for, casting off one's dignity for.

And when a moment later she asked what he was there for, he replied that he was taken by the steady pulse of this town and had gone searching for its heart and found this house in the dunes. This seemed answer enough for both of them.

Nella watched the man and then invited him to go where he may—to sit in her chair, or walk her garden, lie on her bed—so she might glean the workings of his particular clock. And he said sure, and went to the kettle and lit a flame. He went to the record and turned it over. He walked in the dune garden and passed his hand across the leaves of the tended plants. He sat at the table and tapped a tune with his fingers on the seasoned wood. Finally he went to her bed and lay down.

'It's strange?' offered Nella. 'With you, I cannot find a problem.'

'Well I can,' he said.

And he rose and made for her shed, rummaged a little and returned with an oil can. He applied what was necessary, tested the springs—heard nothing—and smiled. Then he rose once more, but slower now, and passed Nella as she stood beautiful in the small hallway, his arm brushing the curve of a shoulder, of a breast, of a belly that was made for children and always had been.

He felt himself blushing and made for the doorway, and the street. And Nella watched him depart and remembered then the orbit of the earth, and day and night, and the fact that life is repetitions—we cannot expect the patterns of our yesterdays to unravel overnight and be knit anew. To ponder otherwise is trouble.

She watched another retreating man reach her gate.

She watched as he paused, bent down, and oiled. And then he turned—sporting the grin of a sweet child—and swung the gate, its silence deafening.

'See?' he called happily. 'It was just the hinges. Nothing more than that.'

And Nella Sands watched him from the doorway, and she knew it now, of course she did.

'Hey,' she said. 'This might sound strange, but are you Treestump? That a name you know?'

The man's gate-swinging slowed, and he watched her now, truly taken by her magic.

'It's a name I had. Not for a long time though—that name died in a war. Just Alistair Mackenzie now. Why's that?'

Nella smiled, heard the kettle whistle, and was gone—propping the screen door open with an empty jar, refilling the kettle to a higher point, and boiling it anew.

# 6

## Conor, the Orphan

I grew up in a home for delinquent kids. The home was on a hill, and the hill had a view of a forest. It was the saddest thing that they never let us visit that forest, sadder than the cold rooms or the bad food or the violence that ran through the place. I avoided the violence, because I was tall from a young age and quiet enough to seem menacing. I never raised a fist to anyone, but to many that looked like restraint, instead of the fear that it was.

The home had a chapel room, from its old days as a hospital probably, or from its days back before that as a prison. And the window behind the altar had the best view of the forest, so I prayed a lot without really praying. Or without praying in the right, godly way. Mine were prayers of escape or of long-lost relatives turning up one day and saying, *We've found you at last*, and loving me, and holding me.

And prayers of the forest. I prayed for the time I'd be old enough to walk out the gate and down to it—climb the trees and find the nests, meet those families I'd imagined for so long. With all the praying I looked like a believer, and that kept me safe too, because religion's an odd language not everyone speaks.

I made friends, which you can do in a place like that no matter what people say about caged animals and their armour. Pat was a lanky kid with bad tattoos all over his arms, and a cigarette always behind his ear. His real name, he told me once, was Vincenzo, after his Italian dad who drove a truck and had sex with his mum one time. He could have been Vince of course, but if you're shedding half a name, it's just as easy to hang up the whole thing. Pat had a big mouth, which would have got him into trouble except he was funny, and dark places need humour, even if it's usually the cruel variety that was one of his brands.

Other kids who walked into the home for the first time either kept their eyes low and humble, or fixed on every face they saw, like they were walking down an aisle in a library reading all the titles.

Pat did something we'd never seen before: he looked back. He actually walked in backwards, arms swinging, studying the outside world as it left him at the gate. Then he turned round to us and saw us all looking, and said really loud: 'Well, thank fuck I'm out of that place.'

It was a good opening line. Most of us appreciated what it held (a nod to an *us* and *them*, with *us* being okay for once) and we smiled. And the ones who wanted to fight him would have anyway so it wasn't a loss really.

When he asked to sit with us, we slid over. When he talked with his hands, we silently forgave him. And when he cracked a joke about our place being nothing compared to the resorts he was used to, we called bullshit but laughed anyway.

Truth was Pat had spent his last night waiting in a car out the front of a motel while his mum bought speed off a pasty-looking guy inside. The cops arrived and Pat tried to drive away. And when he crashed into the side of the reception office they called him in and found out he was only fourteen, that he hadn't been to school in a long time and that he didn't have a lot of family love. And they found him a place here with us.

But what they didn't know, as they sat Pat on the bonnet and checked through his wallet, was that the family love was there in spades—that the object of it was standing in the shadows of a carwash beside the motel right at that moment, eyes twinkling in the moonlight, thankful. What they didn't know was that Pat had been driving since he was six and could have easily backed away, only that wouldn't have stopped the cops heading into the room, wouldn't have distracted them so his mum could run out of it.

A part of love is sacrifice, and though the sacrifices between

39

Pat and his mum only ever went in one direction, that didn't make the love any less. The more she failed, the more he loved, and it would always be that way. Take away the big mouth, the nickname, the real name, the years we knew each other, the years before or after, and that love remained. It was his skeleton, the thing that kept him standing.

I met her once, when she came to visit on the days people did. I was sitting with my social worker, Julie, at the next table and Pat tapped my elbow, introduced us. She looked impatient—like she hadn't planned on me, on this—and we shared polite words quickly. And then we went back to being in separate places, but I kept watching them together—and while everyone else was giving their kid care packages, Pat's mum was asking him for cigarettes, and for anyone he could think of who might have some money to lend her 'cause a thing she'd been sure of had just fallen through and there was no way around it and anyway it wasn't her fault in the first place and, really, she was just clearing up someone else's mess.

And as she was saying all this (in the fake, practised ways junkies do), he stared into her eyes—with love, like she was reading him a bedtime story. Her voice was all raspy but he heard it like it was a poem.

Finally she finished, and he smiled and nodded and wrote down a number for her to call. And then they just sat there, quiet. They passed his last cigarette back and forth, and she looked tired, looked pained for having asked and he looked proud, just proud to be there with her.

And I learnt in that moment that love is a document that has to be translated. It's written in so many languages, and each version you come across you have to learn anew. The word for regret in one love sounds exactly the same as the word for pride in another. And learning any one dialect is an education that takes as long as those two people have known each other.

I was staring at Pat and his mum. And when I finally remembered where I was and looked back, Julie was staring too.

I don't know what was in her head—we never discussed it, even though we discussed a lot. But for me that moment made me feel more like an orphan than ever before. Because sure you can cry for not having a happy family (and I have, often). But to cry for not having a sad one—that hits you in a whole other way.

# 7

## Conor and the Visitor

One day we're in P6, in the school wing, and Ms Knowles says we're going to write a letter to a family member. Which is a terrible exercise seeing as lots of us are orphans, or wish we were, but then Ms Knowles is a terrible teacher so it's not surprising. We all groan and sit down at desks and get started, and the ones who are illiterate just say the words while a support worker writes them down. Pat writes to his mum, a rough-nut called Terry storms out (which kind of says every-thing there is to say), and I write to my aunt Kelly—she doesn't exist but it's easier than explaining that every person in my family is dead and having to talk with Ms Knowles about how that makes me feel.

Then when we've finished our letters, Ms Knowles—having reached new heights of not understanding us and our age and our insecurities—makes every boy sit with a girl and share what we've written. It'd be painful for any teenager, but especially ones who live in a hard place with feigned strength. And she either couldn't see that, which made her stupid, or she could, which made her cruel. And I honestly don't know which it was.

A girl I've never seen before sits down heavily on the chair across from me. She shakes her head at the dumbness of the whole thing and throws her letter on the desk, wanting to get it over with. And I see the letter isn't a letter, but a poem. The poem says:

> *Grief*
> *is the blanket*
> *that the paramedics*
> *put over the survivor's shoulders*
> *And it turns out they never ask for that blanket back*
> *It turns out you wear that blanket the rest of your life*
> *It's pretty ordinary looking*
> *so most people just think it's a shawl*
> *or a wide scarf maybe*
> *But sometimes*
> *when you're walking down the street*
> *or sitting on a bus*
> *or writing a poem*
> *you look up for a second and you see*

*Nearly everyone is wearing a blanket*
*And you kind of feel sorry for the ones who aren't*
*Because yes, life was easier before they put it on you*
*But it keeps you warm*
*It keeps you warm.*

'Who wrote that?' I ask the girl, and she shrugs.

'So's that you then? Does the shrug mean it was you?'

'Where I'm from, a shrug means mind your fucking business.'

'Where are you from?'

'Here. Mind your fucking business.'

Her eyes wander to the window as a bird passes silent in the distance, a line cutting the clear cold air, and I study her face. She looks older than she should, like you can see both her real age and also the wear and tear of history. But she is beautiful. Very delicately beautiful. If her life had been easier, she'd be stunning. But then she wouldn't look like she had a story, and that's half the beauty.

I watch the bird too. 'I've never met anyone actually from town. Usually we all get sent here from somewhere else,' I say.

She shrugs, keeps looking at the sky. Her trackpants sit low and her hips are visible. She notices me staring.

'Sorry,' I mutter.

She just looks down at the page. 'I'm just here for a bit. Was going off the rails so got put in with you lot.'

'That's pretty shit. There's some full-on people in here.'

'Well maybe I'm full-on too.'

44

This time I hold her gaze.

'I'm not really,' she says.

'I kind of figured. From the poem.'

'Was that a clue, was it?'

'A bit, yeah.'

And she smiles with her eyes. And I smile at her smiling.

She says her name is Liz and I say mine is Conor, and she asks about my letter and I could lie but I don't and that surprises me. I tell her about my parents dying in a house fire when I was a baby. How one of them must have put me out on the lawn and then rushed back in for the other, but no one knows which because neither one came out again. And her face does the thing everyone's does when I say that, which is why I don't say that anymore.

Then I'm surprised again because she doesn't say the next thing everyone does which is, *But isn't there anyone else?* She stares out the window again, and says, 'I guess seeing you have no one, you can fill your life with whoever you want now.'

And that's amazing.

I ask Liz who the grief in her poem is for, and who she's written the poem to, and if those two people are the same?

She says a lot of her life these days is about shocking people—how everyone's worried about her, so she kind of feels she should live up to the worry. 'But I don't know. If one day they just change their minds and decide I'm not a worry anymore, then I don't think I will be. Honestly. They'll trust me, and I'll trust that trust and it'll keep going, the same way they're scared now and I just keep scaring them more.' She looks down at the table and runs her hand across it, like she's trying to understand it. 'But how do you switch it? You know? How do you stop worried people worrying, so instead they become calm people getting calmer? What's that moment?'

I tell her I don't know. She looks back at her poem, holding it with two hands like she really wants to find the answer in it, and I look at her the same way. I'm learning something new in that moment—about how someone can attract you accidentally. The sunlight landing perfectly on her face isn't a choice—she's just reading a poem. Her pants don't hang low because she needs me to see her hips—they just settled there when she sat. She makes no effort. And that's beautiful.

A minute later the bell goes. Liz stands up—out of her chair and out of her thoughts. She smiles when she sees me, like I've gone away and come back.

'I'm leaving here soon. So I'll be around town—if you ever want to come looking.'

'Sure.' I shrug with a calmness I don't feel.

And then she walks through the door and is gone, a line cutting the clear cold air.

# 8

## Emma, the Exile

My four days has become four years. I am twenty-three now. A very old person.

In these years I have met no other boats. A few times I have seen them, but always I sailed away quick so nobody would die. It is no bother—I catch the rainwater and I eat the fish. I watch the horizon and I write songs. Ulli left his guitar on the boat and I have learnt to play it. I am a wonderful guitar woman now, truly amazing.

In these years Papa has lived on in his house, I hope, and is not sick anymore, I hope.

The land calls me sometimes, but I ignore it.

Today it is springtime and I am somewhere in the vast

ocean and the sun has come up. The sun has come up on hundreds of dead men, all lying on the sea.

Some are on their backs and some are on their fronts. Some are close in pairs and groups, and some lie very alone, like they did not wish to share their dying with anyone else. One holds a life ring and the life ring says *The Orkney*. This was the name of their ship. The life ring did this man no good though—he too is dead. It is the cold that killed them, I could have told them that. But now I do not have to. They know.

For two days, I sail among them with a long rope, making loops and tying each at the hand. I do this altogether 235 times until there is the longest line of bodies floating behind my papa's fishing boat. I do not know why I have done this. But I do know it feels better than having every man float in his own direction. The sharks come around and nibble at one, and then another—a little bit at one man, the whole body of his friend.

Then I realise the answer and I take the anchor from Papa's boat and tie it to the end of the long line of dead men who were once the crew and passengers of *The Orkney*. I have no need for this anchor—it is for stopping and I cannot stop. So I give it to the men and they disappear below the surface one by one in a long line, each with his one hand out in front of him—*goodbye, goodbye, goodbye.*

They are all sinking down, down to the seafloor where Mama and Paddy Blue Skin and Ulli and his silence (or maybe now his many words) wait to greet them. I write a message for Mama and tie it to the rope, for them to deliver. But I will not tell you what it says—it is words between a daughter and a mama, and you do not need to know.

Then I sail away and return to the things I am good at. Maybe a problem today is people try to be good at too much. They maybe do not achieve this and they get sad. But me, I am good at three things—catching fish, playing Ulli's guitar and killing everyone I meet.

And two of these I could do forever with a smile on my face—honestly, you would not believe my pleasure. But the other one… This is no joy. I wish very much I did not have this talent. Because then, maybe, I could go home.

∞

More years have flowed behind me in the wake of my small boat. I do not know the true number though. First I counted every dawn as it showed up, and every sunset as it went away, making one notch each time in a piece of wood I found on deck.

The wood was the keeper of my history and I was proud of this record I was making. One day I could come home and hold it out to my papa and say: 'Look. This is how many days I sailed alone to keep you alive, old man.'

But one night—a night I did not know was different from any other until it came—the dark was like a tight vest pressing on my chest. And a storm appeared like an angry person shouting at me. And I forgot to be the strong girl that I am (like how I hit a man with a tyre iron when he tried to steal our dog one time when I was nine) and became a crying one, holding my knees, snot running down my chin.

And then I thought, this is a foolish thing and I shouted back to the storm.

'No, fuck you!'

And I stomped across the deck, over and over, roaring that I was not someone made for shouting at, roaring that I was not a person who is weak. And it felt good.

But in my stomping I hit my toe on the piece of notched wood and I realised. Keeping time is weakness, it's something a person does if they fear the world and how it works. Counting your days is desperation. It is you trying to hold on to a small power, against the turning of a giant planet in a giant universe.

So I waved the wood at the storm and showed my teeth (which are not good) and said, 'Here is what I think of this, you fuck!'

And I threw the notched wood into the face of the storm, and I broke the storm's nose.

And the sea ran red. And the storm bowed its head to me and rolled away. This was the worst ever night of my life. And still I beat it.

So now I have no wood and no right memory of the days and months. I can just say I am older now than I was before. Older than when Ulli fell on the jag and rolled into the ocean wrapped in a sheet. But you know this already.

∞

I wake up with the sense of someone looking.

I know it cannot be true, but I imagine a face in my cabin window. It is like after a bell rings, how you still feel the ringing floating in the air for a bit. It is like that. So I creep on deck like a cop in an American movie and there is a woman on my boat. I am alone, far at sea, and now here is a lady.

'Hi,' she says.

'You did not arrive normally. I would have heard you climb on. And you are not wet, so you did not come from the ocean. And I have been to no port, so you are not a stowaway.'

'No.'

The magic woman plays with the zip on her hoodie and looks past me at the sea. I could argue with her but I feel tired so I just sit down.

'You have come to tell me my papa is dead.'

'No.'

'Then…?' Oh.' I am suddenly feeling more tired. 'You are telling me I am dead.'

'No.'

'This is funny. I always think of him, Papa, and if he is alive or if he is not. But I never thought of this.' I am laughing—it is almost like relief. 'That maybe I am the one dying, alone, on a boat. Alone, with a ghost.'

'I'm not a ghost.'

I give her a very serious look. 'And you are honestly not

51

here for me?'

'No.'

'Or my papa?'

'I don't know him.'

'That is good. I think you are like me—I think we are good people not to know.'

She ignores this and stands up, like she is getting ready to go. Even though we are at no place.

'Sail closer to land tonight,' she says.

'I have not been to the land for many years.'

'Not all the way, just closer. Sail closer.'

And then she is gone. Which feels quite normal for some reason. And I make a strange course, one that is pointing to a place instead of away from it. And *this* feels weird—more weird than a woman just now vanishing.

But I am far far out to sea, so even closer to land is still really fucking far away from land and so I am not worried. I go back down to the cabin and go to sleep. I was probably asleep anyway the whole time, but you know what I mean.

∞

I am woken by birds.

This is a danger as birds belong to the shore—unless it is an albatross, and I have seen one twice before and both were special days for my memory. But these birds (there are three) are not albatrosses. Two seagulls stand proud on a coiled rope with their chests puffed up. And one circles above and will not land because the big one below shouts if it comes close and I think that maybe they are bird lovers who are arguing.

I see all this when I climb on deck with sleep crust in my eyes and my tits swinging (it is a hot night and I sleep with nothing). And then I see the next thing, the land!

It is so close, which means I have drifted on a strong current or I have slept for many hours. The sun is high in the sky and so it is the second one—maybe I am in the beginnings of a fever or maybe my brain let me stay in a wonderful dream until it was done. I think back but there is only blur, as it is with dreams. One part of the blur is a mountain but I cannot believe my brain would let me miss half the day for just a mountain.

This land has mountains too—or a big hill. A big bald hill. This land has long beaches as well and I am so close I can see the windows of a house in the dunes. Stretching from the beach is a jetty, and moored to it is a boat no bigger and no smaller than mine. It does the same kind of fishing we do I think, because its nets hang to dry in the sun and I know those kinds of nets.

But the water is warm here so the fish those nets catch are not fish I know. And there are pots on deck so they are interested in crabs too, and we do not catch these. We *did* not catch these—I must remember I have Papa's boat now and if he is living, he must be on land, doing a different job. Maybe a policeman like his papa was.

I have been studying the fishing boat because you always

bring your eye first to what you know, so I almost don't notice the thing I know less—which is other people. A man, carrying a small girl on his shoulders. She is pointing at me and he is looking at me and my tits are out, I realise, and I put on a top that hangs on my washing line (it is just a line but now it holds washing, so you understand what I mean).

They do not look away now though. They still are looking. And I still am looking as well.

The girl's hair is long and messy and her cheeks are not fat and I understand straightaway that her life is like mine, that a good catch means you eat well and a bad catch means you do not, and Christmas is not a lot more special than any other day, and if you receive a small chocolate one afternoon you feel lucky, and the wind whistles through parts of your house, and your clothes were not always your clothes but someone else's before, and you are happy enough but you imagine sometimes what it might be like to have more toys—not like a sadness but more like a little game you play in your head called Rich People.

So yes, I picture my life in her life, but, really, the child I am remembering is Paddy Blue Skin, even if he is a dead boy and she is an alive girl. I see him now on Papa's shoulders because of the way she keeps one hand placed on her papa's head.

When Ulli and I were small and rode like this, we swung our arms, or reached for the icicles that hung from the eaves of the house, or stretched, or did a hundred things. We had no cares and would forget where we were sitting until he spoke

54

and we remembered. Paddy Blue Skin, though, he held on with one hand.

And when we all went to the forest to get wood, he would always need to see one of us with his eyes. He would bend down to pick up the branches, but then stand and look for us again and then bend down again and then look for us again. Of course, because we are family, we made it hard and waited for him to bend down and then jumped behind trees or curled up in ditches. He would stand up and find himself alone with no one in the whole forest or maybe even the whole world except him.

And he would cry and we would laugh, and this was a game that never ended. Until he ended and then the idea of this game left a cold feeling in me, like I was lying in a ditch somewhere in the forest and the snow is pressing against my cheek.

I look at the girl's hand on her papa's head, her hand telling her this is still her papa and will always be her papa and that she cannot be lost. And in my mind I see Paddy Blue Skin suddenly alive again. And maybe this is why I smile.

The man sees me smile, and the man smiles back. My cheeks go hot, I feel it, and I coil a rope beside me that does not need coiling. Looking back to land, I see the man point to the jetty, and the girl put both hands on his head now. She is trying to read his mind through her palms, but minds do not share themselves this way so she is unsure. Unsureness is a feeling she has often—I can see this.

He points again, inviting again. And knowing one million per cent I will never head to shore until I am back at my home, until I am ready, I turn the sails and I head to shore.

# PART TWO

# FLOWING

# 9

## Emma and Conor
## and Anja, the Beginning

After the boat docked, the woman went below deck and was gone a long time.

The man and his daughter weren't sure if she was okay, if she needed help with something or had to do a thing herself. There seemed no right way to find out, so they waited on the jetty, leaning against two posts.

The daughter heard a fish splashing, or maybe a squid, so she lay on her belly and her dad crouched beside her. They watched the shadow of something dark and slow-moving pass beneath the jetty in a wide figure of eight.

'Infinity,' said the girl because this was a word she'd learnt recently.

When they looked up over their shoulders, the woman from the boat was standing on the jetty in the sunshine, a tall silhouette. She'd made no noise so they had no idea how long she'd been there, and from the puzzled look on her face she had no idea either. She stared past them, at the shadow under the sea, and waved to it. Noting the pair's expression, she grew self-conscious and said, 'I know some ones who live down there.'

And it was not an answer.

'You have an accent,' said the girl.

'We all have accents,' said the woman. 'But I know what you mean. I am from the north.'

'Far away?' asked the girl.

'Infinity away.' And she smiled. 'It is a very good word, I think.'

There is a comfort that comes from not having to explain, and the trio found this comfort with each other. With the woman shouldering only a small rucksack, they left the jetty and walked across the sand in silence.

The man collected driftwood as they went, so the woman did too, and this went unacknowledged, in the nicest way. The girl turned her attention to the tide and walked exactly its line but a metre higher, always keeping a perfect distance from the waterline—a tightrope walker, but without the bravery.

Finally, the girl veered away from the sea and ran up through a gap in the dunes to the path that led to a garden (coastal plants—greys and yellows and whites). The man paused at a garden gate and turned, waiting with a patient chivalry. The woman (who had known patient men but no chivalrous ones) flicked a smile as she navigated the dunes, the running girl her north star. At a point, she heard the song of a bird unknown to her, and was stilled, eyes wide in search of it.

'A honeyeater,' stated the man, and he took the lead.

So first the girl and then her father and finally a washed-up foreigner reached the house. It was small and solid and its chimney smoked and its windows were warm like eyes. The man dropped his armload of wood on a pile that needed no additions, and the woman did the same.

He ruffled his daughter's hair and pointed, and she nodded, heading into the house and then appearing in a kitchen window, boiling the kettle. The man pulled out a pouch and sat on a low bench on the porch. Leaning back against the weatherboards, he rolled a cigarette.

'You have one of those behind your ear already,' said the woman, and then immediately wished to unsay it, as he smiled and presented the cigarette to her, placing the old one in his mouth. She took it and when he held out a lighter she lit it. And then Conor the orphan and Emma the Greek sat side by side, smoking cigarettes and drinking the tea that Anja brought them.

∞

After cigarettes have been smoked (first one and then several) and cups of tea have been emptied, and the sun has gone down and the plants have grown tall, night falls.

It isn't bitterly cold, and a fire crackles, so the man and his child and the fisherwoman stilled sit outside in front of the house and listen to the push and pull of waves beyond the dunes. Emma the Greek, only hours ashore, hasn't yet made peace with inertia and appreciates the sound of the sea as poor but pleasing cousin to its roll beneath her boat.

If she closes her eyes she can picture herself back upon it, and Conor and Anja watch her do this, body leant against the weatherboard, faintest movement hinting at an ocean within. They spy each other spying, one raising an eyebrow and the other nodding the smallest nod, a fluent dialogue between quiet people.

'I am feeling being back on the sea,' explains Emma with eyes still closed and they learn she speaks their language—the language they speak without speaking.

Over the past hours, Emma the Greek has told the man and his daughter about the ocean and her adventures—about boats that sank and a mother dead and brothers dead and others dead. If they'd had a question she'd given detail. If they were silent she'd pushed on. And it felt like a shedding—like standing on a porch when you've run through the rain, and stepping out of boots, and stripping off each layer, and shaking loose your hair, and wiping down your face with a sure, strong hand before you open the door and step into a warm room. It has seemed that she couldn't enter into that warm-room comfort until every tale was told, until every memory—still dripping—was hung upon its hook.

'And then...I am here at now.'

She pauses, surprised by her arrival in the present. She throws the last of her cold tea into the darkness and stands up. Stamps her feet to wake her blood. Stretches her arms to crack her bones.

'You are wonderful listeners. I hope every person who is carrying too many stories will meet someone like you and you. And if the story in my stories—if the thing Ulli said of me meeting you and you meeting death is true now—I am so sorry. I do not want to kill bad people. But I one-hundred-per-cent do not want to kill good ones.'

Again one raises eyebrows and the other nods, roles reversed this time, her asking, him answering. And just in case Emma hasn't grasped their unspoken language yet, Anja speaks.

'In this house, every night before bed, we tell stories. Mostly Dad tells them because he's older and knows more, but sometimes I do because I'm younger and I can imagine better. Plus he has a bookshop full of stories written already. But some are just his. And some, we don't know where they come from.

'And you, Emma the Greek—we don't know where you come from either. I mean, you told us. But that's just the story telling the story. It's not like we don't believe you—I do, and I think Dad does.'

Again, the smallest of nods.

'It's just...you can't really say what a story means until it's over. And you're not over. Your brother Ulli is and so his story about you carrying death makes sense to him. *Made* sense for him.'

Emma the Greek looks into Anja's eyes, and then into the fire, and then back into the girl's eyes.

'But we're meeting you in the middle of your story,' Anja continues. 'And you're meeting you in the middle of your story. So you can only guess it's about carrying death. And maybe it is. But maybe it's not, too. And maybe, it doesn't matter. Maybe arriving on our jetty just closes that book. Maybe you get a new story now. Maybe it's a happier story. Or a sadder one. Maybe we're in it. Maybe that's good. But what I think is that none of us three knows what the story is yet.'

And the little girl finishes talking and looks to her dad. And the man smiles a small, warm smile that creases his eyes and means *You are speaking with a knowledge I didn't teach you.* Which is a parent's greatest pleasure in the whole wide world.

Anja rises and waves a small goodnight and goes inside. Conor rises too, takes the empty cup from the fisherwoman and looks at the dunes. He turns, eyes warm, and says, 'I think you washed up in the right place.'

Then he enters the house, leaving the door open behind him.

And Emma the Greek is alone by the fire, alone for the first time since stepping onto land. Her clothes—damp for so many years—have dried, salt crusted into their seams. Her cup has been taken inside and placed upon a sink. Her stories have been aired, her demons named, her explanations given. Her history has been told.

And a history—she sees now as she watches the embers blink at her—isn't precious in itself, only, really, in the person it makes. That person is the one a father and daughter invited into their home. And their home is here, and their lives are here, and she sees in that moment both can hold her—and will hold her—for years to come.

But not all she carries on her boat as well. Those are provisions of the sea, flung hurriedly from one sinking vessel to another over decades and generations—memories and nicknames and keepsakes and tin cans and sorrows. Anything not salvaged has sunk—and too much has sunk—so too much value has been given to what is left.

So on the fishing boat those things will stay, and to the jetty the boat will be moored—she won't unlash knots and set her history floating out to sea, but she won't be surrounded by it either. She'll enter this house and climb into the warmth of a bed, and the comfort of a love, and the eventual memories of a child.

And Emma the Greek will continue to hear the sea calling, of course she will.

But she will ask that it call her by a new name.

∞

I walk outside of the house, and the morning is cold—not like cold at home, but a cold the people from here would notice.

I had sex with the man last night, quiet because his girl was sleeping in a close-by room. It was very good, better than with the boy from the first time, and with the three after that—one was clumsy, one was rough and called me terrible things, one had fear in his eyes. This time, the sex was the sex. Conor was not trying to prove a thing or explain a thing or forget someone else. When he held my hip or my tit, I held his hand holding me. When he stood up, I knelt. When I lay back on the bed with my knees wide, he smiled at my pussy and ate it and I pulled his hair. And he kissed me after and I tasted myself.

I woke up early, which I usually do not do, and I watched him. He sleeps with an arm over his head like he dreams of running through a fire. And I put on bits of clothing I found in the dark—some his, some mine—and walked down the wooden stairs and none of them squeaked. I made coffee but in a quiet way, so Conor could sleep and Anja too.

Then I came out the front door, wearing a big woollen jumper belonging to the man, with his cup full of his coffee, looking for one of his cigarettes. And I found his daughter.

She is sitting on the porch writing in a book and this makes perfect sense—that she is a writer, or a one-day writer. It is why she tries to read her papa's thoughts through his head. Like why Paddy would try to find us in the forest with his big eyes. It is wanting to know everything. Only, not by doing—by borrowing.

She looks up at me and smiles. Maybe she heard the sex and is okay, or maybe we were quiet enough. I hope the second.

And I see that beside the book on her lap, there is a coin. It is large and old and the kind that is heavy. I don't ask and Anja doesn't offer but I know it is okay, and I pick it up, turn it over.

'A coin like this is very valuable,' I tell Anja, to make her be amazed and silent.

'Mm. So are a thousand of them,' says the girl. And she reaches down and moves one of the porch boards, then points to a giant pile of coins in the darkness below.

And I am amazed, and silent.

But then after a bit I remember words again.

'Where did you find these?'

And she smiles at me, and her eyes tell me she is a writer already, that she has borrowed all my thoughts already. And she says, very simple, 'A bird showed me.'

# 10

## The Widow and the Wealth

Here is where I keep a vase of flowers. Small, simple ones—ones that pop up around the garden and catch my eye. I tell the gardener that too (he has a crippled leg). 'Do not plant only a single type. Scatter seeds as you will and see what takes hold. And once some have lived and some died, then I will make my own assessments. Some I shall pick and arrange in vases, others I shall leave for Nature to display upon her own table.'

I like that sort of thing: not making too many choices at the beginning, but rather at the end. When we see what we are left with, and decide what to do from there.

This was Henry's study.

A man came here with a dog the other day. He said he was

here to put up wallpaper, and the walls do need it, that is not a lie. So I let him in. Or I got Betty to let him in. And, do you know, he brought the dog in too. Well, I was shocked, I won't lie. But Betty, the girl, went red as a robin's bust and shouted at the poor Irishman. Betty protects my dignities—the house, my sensitive manners—in a way she does not protect herself. And what I mean by that is she fell pregnant once. But it died.

Henry would not have minded the dog entering. He had a love for dogs, a real profound love. He was not a fan of people, and dogs are not people, so it all worked very well. And given his custom, I would have probably let the Irishman traipse inside with the hound. But then seeing Betty scream so on my behalf—well it would have been rude to undermine her. To let it stay when she was yelping like a banshee would have boded well for no one I'm sure. So the dog stayed out in the cold, and the man ascended a ladder and hung sheets of paper—a lovely burnt-yellow hue.

As he did that, and as Betty fussed about below— complaining of mud on his shoes and an odour he possessed, in a way that made it very obvious she loved him—I imagined Henry leaving them to it, letting himself out the front door, and sitting quietly with the dog.

So I did this. Though it went against every part of my nature, I tiptoed out before Betty or one of the other servants could dissuade me. And there it was, tied to the rail. I gathered my dress, and I sat on the bottom step alongside it. I sat there, so we were face to face, and I patted it, as I believe Henry would have done. The ribs were exposed, and I was not surprised, as the poor have poor dogs, I do understand this.

And then it bit me.

It bit me on the shoulder—though I imagine the plan was my neck—and it held me like that. It didn't growl. And I didn't yell. Instead we both sat there in silence, as the fangs sank further in and I felt warm blood running down my back. We sat like that, as snow began to fall.

Finally the door opened and Penny—a subordinate of Betty's—came out with dirty water to discard and saw us. And she screamed like a siren, and then there were many feet running, and the Irishman took a large stick and beat that dog off me. He beat it to death. But it held on to my shoulder for as long as it could. And it was silent all the time. And so was I. And we watched each other. And I saw the brightness of its eyes give out. I saw its eyes go cold.

It is a story I would tell Henry were he here.

∞

He gave me one week in bed, Doctor Salter did. Salter is obscenely overweight which I've always found odd in a man of medicine. But perhaps that is the sacrifice. He keeps the rest of us in good shape while forsaking his own. One day he will clutch at his heart and keel over, while we that were healed by him remain. It is almost noble. Grotesque, but noble.

Betty changed my dressings just as the fat man showed her,

and she did it well, dabbing at the stitches Salter had sewn into me. (So feminine a thing for a man to do. I remember smiling at the sight and he asked what was pleasing me and I said, 'Oh nothing.')

The man who owned the dog—who owned it and who also killed it—is in prison now. This is sad, of course. He is a man, not a dog. He did not bite my shoulder. But the price of the injury, it was decided, was his to pay. I protested a little, when they told me. But only a little. Everything has to end somewhere after all. It's not always exactly the right place, but it is a place. If it is of consolation to him, the prison sits on a hill I believe, so I assume there is a view of some kind. Are prisoners afforded views? Do their cells have windows or just something more akin to vents? The good prisoners get windows perhaps. I assume he is a good prisoner. He seemed nice enough.

The day I emerged from my bedroom, Betty was waiting for me and she looked so serious—standing there in the hall, hands crossed in her lap, a sad look on her ridiculous face.

'Ma'am...'

You could tell she'd rehearsed it—she did a little cough and everything.

'Ma'am, it's been a year.'

She said it as if I wasn't aware.

'Today it is a year and we were wondering—I mean, I was and then others too...it's just, the house. And all his things. All his things being in the house. In the exact same places he left them. Well...of course it'll always be his house. But...but it's yours too. Isn't it? First it was his. And then you had it together—for that time, for that happy time, happy time cut too short. And now it's…in a way…yours. Your house. And I thought—we thought—it could do with a wee change, maybe?

'Like how we got in that yellow wallpaper, the day of the… seeing how yellow's your colour, and how it wasn't so much his colour but now that's not so much of an issue. And we thought, if the wallpaper went up all right, then maybe…maybe we could give everything a…a good old spring-clean. And some of his things. His hat there by the door, his overcoat, the pipe there where it lies on that round low table in the library. Well maybe those things could—'

I hit Betty so hard in the face her glasses bounced off the nearby wall.

I didn't slap her. I wasn't cautioning her. My fingers were curled into my palm, my knuckles were my knuckles, and I swung them into her freckled cheek. Her nose immediately bled, and the side of her eye began to swell in that very instant. It was astonishing how quickly it occurred, as though some chemical process had been ready to go, just waiting for permission—and this was the result.

Betty was a good girl and she didn't make a sound, other than a small gasp which she drew back into herself. She just nodded and walked away, trying to be as mannered as she could. At a point along the hallway, she tottered sideways a little and fell into the wall. She caught her weight with one hand and that hand was bloodied and that blood stained my paintwork, so that is a job for later. But for that moment she carried on around the corner.

We have not spoken about Henry's things since and, honestly, that's a good thing.

∞

When the will was read, it was the circus one would expect. His children were there, sour-faced to a one, three of them older than me which I know makes them incredibly angry. I smiled at them. Gave a little wave across the room. Not mature, no, but it was what I did.

We waited a year before the reading, in accordance with a clause stipulating this should any small chance of his being alive remain. And there was indeed an ambiguity—his body was his body, and it was found and it was frozen. But his face was gone. The mortar that ended Henry's life took his face with it, so there existed a small possibility, a *what if?*

Not in my mind of course—I felt him die the moment it happened. I had been sitting in a chair, reading a book, and suddenly I bent forward like a horse had kicked me. And later I found out that was the very moment he ended. So I knew, absolutely. But that type of explanation does not fly with the legal profession, and I appreciate this. So, a year we waited.

The house I kept. Most of everything I kept. The children roared and raged. Some business folk did too—they wailed about promises he'd made. Waving these words in the air like

73

petulant gamblers with dead tickets at the end of a horserace. Business is ink, I could have told them, just as Henry had once told me. Business is ink, not handshakes or smiles or blood-lines. Take a promise to your bank manager and see which account he would suggest it be placed in. He would laugh as it fluttered out the window on the breeze.

One thing was comical—a wedge of land, a distant uncon-sidered wedge. Only this he left to family, to a great-nephew, a child of a child of a brother. A failure. Such was the joke of it—one I enjoyed while the others in the room looked around in shock, poor things. The man was a shell of a man, broken by life. A murderer no less! Yes. Yes, I said it.

Henry, it transpires (in a letter left for my beloved eyes only), had charted this man's course over years. Had indeed steered it: a bank position unceremoniously tossed, a manu-factured debt dropped in its place, a wife whispered to of indiscretions—all false. Little things, but cumulative. It was an amusement, watching one life collapse as his own ascended. So many shared genes but (for some reason a scientist may deduce—a brain scientist maybe, one who unpicks minds like knotted fishing nets) their resilience was entirely opposite, their lives poles apart.

And when the land below the prison came up for sale, and Henry had spent an evening musing on that land, on this great-nephew's eyes staring out at it, year after wretched year from the prison on the hill, he bought it. Of course he did. And so set in place a moment of divine transference. Written

74

into a will, a clause—that whenever Henry's life ceased, so the stranger's would begin. He would be pardoned (Henry had power), he would walk out of a jail and down a hill and onto a patch of earth that was miraculously his.

And the bet Henry wagered with himself was that a man is a man. Was that he would squander it all, sell off the paddocks piece by desperate piece and end up scavenging on a beach maybe, walking into the sea maybe, a carcass found bobbing blue and fish-eaten. Those are the games Henry played, games others would not understand. Which is why we shared a life so well.

Which is why I shall never pack his overcoat away, or sell his hat, or move his pipe and spectacles. I will keep Henry's museum. I will be Henry's museum. I will grow old in our house, beside our things, his and mine and no one else's.

I will keep Betty until she is useless (though she does have stamina—I am making my own bets with the gods about that girl). I will get a dog maybe and show it my scar. I will watch the great-nephew, watch him have and then have not. I will scatter seeds and see what takes hold. And once some have lived, and some died, then I will make my own assessments.

# 11

## The Widow and the Founder

She sailed into town. Not by sea, but by road.

The grandness of her buggy caught every eye—the finery of the vehicle, the sombreness of the large horse drawing it, the tallest hat on the short man driving, the whip cracks he delivered without any need, an opulence of cruelty. Every farmer bearing witness hated him and every one of them swallowed that hate.

On the leather seats behind the driver sat two passengers, straight-backed and distinct. One was tall and porcelain, shrouded in a widow's veil, taking in both nothing and everything, as the wealthy somehow can. Beside her, a slight bonneted thing—she had on a widow's blacks too, but only to serve the grief of her lady.

They arrived by the road that curved around Prisoners' Hill, the road from the west. At a point in the woods (known these days as Feasters' Fork) it joined with the road that curved from the other side. And then these two tributaries funnelled into one, the grand labour that had been shaped by every hand for miles around. Main Street was a straight arrow fired to the ocean, its flint a jetty that pierced the water. The local children loved running the length of the wooden boards and flinging their sunburnt forms out over the brine, the shrieks hanging off them, little Icaruses all.

The widow stared straight down Main Street with regal poise, while her maid-girl gawped sideways, as a commoner could, at the neatly painted shops one after another on the left, the bucolic river wending silently between apple orchards on the right. Every bird perched on the rooftops followed the procession with a wary eye.

At a point, with only the smallest gesture from the widow, the travelling party stopped. The cruel driver jumped down and unfolded a step. The dutiful maid bustled to earth and held out a hand. The lady then stood to her full height and alighted step by clicking step, feet small and pointed.

Everyone in that town was proud of that town. Of what they'd carved into the dirt and raised from the foundations. Of the colours they'd painted the businesses they'd built. But still everyone in that town lowered their gaze when receiving hers. It was nothing to feel bad about, just as avalanches aren't. They are bigger than us, and they occur.

'What has happened here?' The widow threw her question at Cam Peterson, caught now beside the tavern door, bruised hat in hand.

'In what...? How, like?' were the feeble syllables he mustered.

'This was not this last year—there was no town where we are standing.'

'Oh. Oh right. Yeah. I mean, yes. No. No there weren't one. Wasn't.'

Bored, she walked away from the young man, an egg cracked but discovered to have no yolk inside. Betty, trotting behind, offered him a small conciliatory smile.

Agnes Clyde stepped proudly out of the trading post door—but not down off its porch, as she knew she needed the height to keep her pride in place. 'It's our new town, ma'am. Services every farm ten miles each way along the coast, it does.'

The widow raised eyebrows and nodded, impressed in the most mocking of ways.

'Well what a magic trick that is! A town just pulled from a hat. Plonked right down beside the sea. Voila!' She lowered her voice. '*Voila* means "There it is".'

'I know what *voila* means.' Agnes hadn't known, but she covered well.

'And the one who owned this land—is he a magician? Did he do a disappearing act? Have you good people of "the farms ten miles each way along the coast" managed to wrest it from him somehow?' She raised innocent hands. 'And no judgment on you if so. That's business.'

'We wrested nothing,' growled Agnes (who was being put to the test with unknown words but battled valiantly). 'The fella owned this land still owns this land. Course he does. It's his.'

'Ah.' The widow nodded reverently, as one humoring a child. 'I stand corrected then. Well, would you be an absolute angel and tell me his whereabouts?'

Agnes bit her tongue (already she knew she'd be asked about this exchange for years to come and wanted her performance to be worthy of the story). Not breaking eye contact, she extended a firm arm and finger out to her left.

'He's sitting on the end of the jetty.' She smiled coolly. 'That's the salty thing, pointing out to sea.'

'Really, dear?' The widow smiled back, considering Agnes' arm. 'I thought that was you.'

Battle won, the widow turned and marched oceanward, her maid-girl scurrying behind her.

∞

Isaac was sitting on the bench. He sat there often of an afternoon, smoking his rolling tobacco—a habit picked up inside, of course, where it served the role of commerce more than vice. But out here, smoking was simply a pleasant way of idling, which suited this chapter of his life well.

He enjoyed staring out to the ocean, which was not his, while knowing that all that lay behind him was. A year before when stepping into the world (and the fourteen incarcerated before that, and the five in turmoil before them, and even truly the first lot before anything) he would never have guessed it so. That such a life might exist. But it could, it did. A pleasant thing to muse on, beside the sea, with a cigarette, under a noonday sun.

'You are the owner of this town.'

Her voice demanded his attention, so he did not turn.

'I am the owner of nothing,' Isaac said to the horizon. 'This place was built by friends and me to fit my friends and me. Are you a traveller?'

'I am an investor. I am indeed your investor.'

Out of curiosity he turned.

'You are far too beautiful, and also far too alive, to be my great-uncle. But—ah yes—there is your black veil. You are his love left behind. Pardon me, I do not know your name?'

The widow smiled and he understood he was not to learn it today, so he nodded his acceptance of this. Placing his hands on knees he went to stand, but she shook her head and bade him stay where he was. Gliding rather than walking, she reached the bench and sat beside him, her skirts ballooning then deflating around her.

Both watched the waves and not each other.

'I expected to find nothing here. You have made a go of it, I see.'

'Well he gave me a gift—you gave me a gift. Seems only right it not be squandered.'

She shook her head. 'No talk of rightness please. You did not build this town for us. To honour us. Honour him.'

He dragged on his cigarette, shrugged. 'All right, then. A town needed founding and so a founder I became.'

Isaac looked at her, considering. 'And now? Have you come to take it from me? Or share a part of it? Or collect a rent or something similar?'

She laughed, and it was not kindly. 'I have so much. More than you will ever have. If each of your new roads spawned twenty new roads, and those new ones did the same, still I would have more than you. No, I simply visited to bear witness. To see how you were getting on.'

The founder finished his cigarette and opened a small metal tin. He crushed the ember to nothing with his fingertips, registering no pain, and then deposited the butt inside.

'And you just said it yourself: you expected to find nothing here. So your journey today was to meet me as a failure. One could even speculate, that this entire exercise—of bequeathing me the land—was built around the expectation of failure that would follow.'

A particularly large wave broke and they both cast their eyes towards it. A long silence settled.

Waiting a discreet distance behind, the girl and the driver shifted their weight uncomfortably. An apple barge, laden, shunted out of the estuary into the open sea and headed west for a market along the coast.

The founder turned to the widow. 'You are not arguing my point.'

She smiled. 'You are not worth the argument. Yes, Henry did the things you said, for the reasons you said. Yes, I travelled here to find you fallen, and so to feel a little better about his significant absence by your wholly unimportant existence. Yes, you have surprised me with what I find here today. And no, I wish for nothing from it. In fact.'

She gestured behind her and the driver nodded and hurried back along the jetty to the buggy, lifted a leather cover at its back and heaved out a small chest, then returned wheezing to the bench, where he laid his heavy load at the pair's feet. He stood up, ruddy and proud of his efforts. Neither the widow nor the founder acknowledged him, so he nodded again and shuffled back to his place.

'All right, I'll bite. What's your cargo?'

'It's not mine. Not anymore. It sits here, on your jetty, in your town, built by your friends and you, to fit your friends and you. The chest holds wealth. A great deal of wealth.'

And she placed a key on the bench between them.

He ignored it, simply tapping the chest with his foot. It was solid and unmoving.

'And what if I don't want it?'

'Why would you not?'

'Because it is another escalation in your game. You are unhappy I have prospered, so you offer this—you wish me to jump at the coins, like a cat clawing at light reflected off a piece of glass. It is wealth to hurt me, not help me.'

She stood and looked at him. 'So odd. You are the only person I have met who thinks like a cruel rich man, just as well as my cruel rich man. You do it so convincingly, I suspect you may be the very article?'

The founder nodded and rose. 'We all are everything.' He smiled, paying the key no mind, and walked back along the jetty.

'Get your man to load it back on the buggy and deliver it to another fool,' he called over his shoulder. 'This one has a haircut to get.'

Isaac winked a small wink at the maid as he passed her by. Then he was gone. She raised her eyebrows imploringly at the driver and he ran back to the bench and stooped down to seize the chest.

'Leave it,' said the widow, and she walked away from the sea, and from the key lying on the bench.

Confused, but also used to being confused by his employer, he did as he was told and rushed after her gliding skirts. He looked back a number of times at the vast abandoned wealth in bewilderment, as though at any moment the chest might grow legs and chase them over the boards.

But it did not. And the trio drove away in the buggy.

Curious locals eyed the chest (close but not too close).

Night fell.

The chest of riches lay still on the jetty.

Next morning, urged by all, the founder walked back to the bench and sat. Every citizen stood around him (this was a good test for the jetty—it held them all). The key lay beside him on the bench where the widow had left it.

'If what you say is true, it's wealth enough to build this town once over,' mused McSweeney.

'But if what I say is true,' Isaac countered, rolling another cigarette, tin balanced on his knee, 'then this chest is Pandora's. Open it up and all the problems of the world will tumble out. Plus, we don't want a second town—we have a perfectly good first one.'

'It's just...it's money,' said Agnes. 'And money's a thing you need. It stops hungry folks being hungry and heals the sick ones and everything like that.'

Many nodded, he too.

'I have no answer there. Besides, my opinion weighs precisely as much as anyone else's. Foodwise, I'll just say there seem crops enough and stores enough to see us through many seasons. Healingwise, I trust our Dr Callen and his apothecary there beside the butcher. And lifewise—well, I've seen more good folks toppled by too much than not enough. But this is a jetty, not a pulpit, and I am a landowner, not a preacher. So do what you will.'

And, again, he turned and walked back along the jetty, back to his home, a small sturdy thing he'd started building in the dunes on the Coast Road.

Sitting at his kitchen table (a sentimental keepsake from

that first feast) and looking out of the broad seaward window, the founder ate his morning meal and watched the townsfolk considering the chest. Sometimes one fellow would raise his chin and say something big, and others would nod or tut in response. Sometimes a few folk would form a huddle and seem to be unpicking the minutiae of the problem. Sometimes a brave someone would come forward and pick up the key. Each time it was put back. And never did anyone open the chest.

Eventually everyone walked away, back to work and school and lives and the big deep questions that they pondered as they went about other things. And at odd times over the next while, people would return—alone or in a pair or as a small mob— witnessed by the founder at his kitchen window. And they'd study the chest, as though it would, at any moment, explain itself to them.

The key now hung on a small length of string someone had fixed to the bench. It gathered salt and tapped against the hardwood in the breeze.

The widow drove past from time to time, first a week later, then a month, then a couple more. Everyone closed their shutters along Main Street when she rolled by, and an eeriness hung in the air as though her black veil had draped itself over every tree and shop.

She'd stop at the jetty's end, observe the chest, bid her driver turn, and depart the way she'd come.

∞

I am up late one night, unable to sleep, hungry, and so eating a sandwich of dense cheese and sweet pickle, elbows resting on my table, staring out to sea, when she arrives in a new capacity. The driver is absent, the buggy too. She simply walks, as any commoner might but, still, she is anything but. Her maid, loyal by night just as by day, walks a pace behind, grumbling at the puddles.

This time, the widow steps onto the jetty. Her tiny feet find each board and avoid the spaces between, her eyes fix ever ahead. The maid-girl is less fortunate and totters fearfully on the jetty. I snuff my candle, watch it all, sandwich held halfway to my mouth, then abandoned on the plate.

I sense her decision to concede the battle, and it warms me like a bath in deepest winter. Her villainy has been conquered—and it is I who am the conqueror. But I wonder (quietly to myself in the homely darkness) if this is cause for concern. Can an evil person be bested only by someone more evil still? Or is it the other way—a great goodness in me that balances her bad? But even this thought suggests something murky.

Torn, unsure of whether I am a just man sitting in his kitchen or a ruthless one, I bite into my sandwich. I wait to see her take her winnings and—in so doing—lose.

∞

There is a wind up as I make my way over the boards. The briny air ruffles me, pulls my skirts against my legs and then lifts them away like it cannot make its mind. It chills my extremities. It makes my veil whip, Henry slapping my face even in his absence. Finally a gust tears it from my skull and sends the black gauze high and billowing over the waves, a dark bird flying across the Styx. Betty gasps as though it is an omen, the idiot.

We reach the end and stare down at the chest. Its latch and hinges are already corroding, the sea a better lockpick than any human hand. One firm boot would send the lid flying now. But this is unnecessary—the key (rusting also) hangs only a foot away, on the bench above the waves.

'How exactly do we get it back, Ma'am?'

Betty's shadow stretches across the jetty in the moonlight, a sleeker version of her form.

'We don't, my dear.'

And while, initially, I'd imagined bidding her do the deed, I now find myself kneeling down and heaving the chest with a strength I never doubted. I stand up, bearing the chest, and take three noble strides forward—then send it crashing into the sea below.

I stand back and rub rusty residue from my gloved palms, proud of my victory.

'But Ma'am…' stammers Betty. 'Now…now no one has it? Now it is lost to all.'

'Hush, stupid girl. It is mine. I have won it.'

'But…it is on the seabed now? You do not even swim.'

'The first true thing you've said in a long time,' I mutter to the wind, and go to walk away.

And Betty stands, unmoving, in front of me.

The moon is out. The key bangs incessantly against the bench. Betty looks down at her hands, confused, as though asking them a question.

And then she places them against me. Against my chest.

I stare at them. I understand them.

I smile.

A push. And I am sent backwards, all the wind knocked from me, all the wind carrying me high and billowing over the waves.

A dark bird.

∞

The water, bursting open and then closing, claims its prize and carries on undeterred.

The girl who is now a murderer stands a moment, long hair blowing in the wind, eyes locked on the sea and its secret held.

She discards her funereal coat, revealing a pale servant dress beneath, her forced mourning instantly ended with this new death.

She looks at my window, at me, I am sure of it.

And then she walks back along the jetty, white as the moon.

# 12

## Isaac's Garden

I am planting a garden around my house in the dunes when she comes.

I like the sea. I like its smell and I like its sound. I like the way it keeps time. I like how it communes with the sky—how much the heavens exist in its depths. It reflects the stars, and heeds the moon, and makes the rain, and drowns the setting sun. The sea is a wonderful neighbour, so I built where I built. But sand is not such fertile ground, and sand pervades. A garden was sacrificed for all the shore might offer, but I had still come away with a bargain.

So for nigh on two years, I enjoyed all I did. As the town grew behind my house, as the jetty was built in front of it. As a woman was drowned before my eyes, and another liberated in that same act. As my reputation evolved, as I was embraced, as my past was eroded by the waves (which eat at history as they do all things), a new life formed for me.

And then it was winter again. No one really likes winter. It is a season when one thinks about the past (when it was warmer) or the future (when the warmth will return). Its job is to remind us that life has befores and afters—that is the point of winter.

Of course there were times of joy. When a family had me to their farm for a long, laughter-filled dinner. When a wedding or a wake or a christening called us together and we rejoiced in our town, spilling out of the tavern and onto the streets beneath the moon's chill stare. Those times were pleasures.

But now the wheel has spun once more—Kepler's grand ellipse repeated over—and here I am sitting on my cold porch again, the winter sea white again, the beach a void, the windows of the town shuttered. But winter is only being winter, so I can not speak ill of it. It wears no false clothing. Spring though— its gloating youth striding into view—this is the real tyranny.

Spring should be a spectacle, and if you inhabit the coun- tryside it is. Lambs are spring. Blooms are spring. Were my home built by the woods, then to see these pleasures would have been as simple as stepping through a door, parting a curtain, walking onto a porch, mug of tea in hand.

So Nature bedamned, I decide—come this time next year, a garden will be in bloom. The sands can protest. The sea can roar. Nautical winds can tear at leaves, mermaids and dead sailors drag themselves across the beach and poison with their songs and hexes all I sow. Still I shall prevail.

And so, I am planting a garden when she comes. I lean on a spade and watch her.

'It is you. Who I handed matches to once upon a time.'

'I lit one of the candles on your long tables at the feast in the forest, yes.'

'Not *my* long tables—they belong to the town. Walk up that main street behind you, you'll find three of them in the tavern. One is now the butcher's chopping block—that one's purple with old blood now, has a mean smell. One you can buy sugar over at the goods store—Mr Carroll, he leans on that one. But, true'—I point behind me with an earthy thumb—'one of them is mine. It stands in there with just one plate on it.'

'Just the one?'

She looks at the wall of the house, as though with magic eyes to see through the timber. 'You've seen me one other time.'

'Have I?'

'I was on the jetty. You must have forgotten.'

I shrug. 'It was night-time.'

She swings my gate lazily and it squeaks a small protest.

'So you remember the hour, but not me.'

'Well. The brain's a funny thing. Smoke?'

I set the spade a little in the sand so it holds itself as I walk away. I sit down on a low bench on my porch, lean back against the wall, and pull the tin from my waistcoat pocket. She walks up the path and sits beside me—I feel the slight give as wood flexes. The fire of a single match serves us both, hers first as is the way with a lady, even one who is a murderer.

For a time we just breathe smoke in and out, like a conversation visible but silent on the spring wind.

'When I pushed her into the sea'—she pauses to pick a strand of tobacco from her tongue—'she gave me no challenge, even smiled as if knowing the thing we were doing before I did. She was always very clever, as the cruel can be.'

The spade gives up and falls gently onto the bed of sandy earth. A wagtail perched on a branch close by darts off and finds the gatepost instead.

'So you did not come to the jetty to kill her that night?'

'Ha. That sounds like a choice. My life with her held no choices—if she went to a place, I went there too. If she lost a husband, I put on a veil. If she was having a bad day, then... so was I.'

There is a whole world in her words, and I let her sit in that world. She does not seem angry or remorseful. Just aware that a life is a chaptered thing and some of those chapters are good and some are terrible. But soon you turn a page and find a new first word, a new season, the earth reset.

'You looked at me. I had snuffed my candle but still somehow you knew I was watching. You looked me square in the eyes, as I sat at my one-plate table.'

She shakes her head.

'It wasn't then. I knew it earlier—when you were on your

jetty bench, arguing with my lady and being stubborn as a mule about the chest—I knew her fate sat a little in your hands. So I knew her death would involve you too.'

I get my tobacco tin, set it on my knee, press the remainder of a cigarette into nothing and shut the butt away. 'So are you cleaning house?' I ask. 'I am the only witness to her ending. Am I then next to be ended?'

'You don't seem scared.'

'Intrigued more than anything.'

'That's a thing she'd have said.'

'Well, that doesn't bode well for me, given how you dispatch her kind.'

She ignores me and flicks her spent tobacco into my seedling garden, a glowing arc dying in a waiting furrow.

She looks at me, properly views me up and down, and smiles. 'You are no good to me dead.'

'Phew. So am I good to you alive?'

'I don't know.'

The smile I feel on my face is unbidden. I'm like a schoolboy again, like the child I was a thousand years ago.

Her magic works then, she vanishes the timber wall we lean on, and together we topple back. We end up lying on the cabin floor.

I rise on an elbow and watch her. Her hair is knotty tendrils spread all directions. Cheeks flushed, freckles out, eyes bright and finding the ceiling. Her chest heaves with a reclaimed breath and her breasts sit as they may, one flatter and pointing to heaven, the other draped towards me. Her thatch glistens with warmth, tight ringlets of hair, and I run my fingers through it. She says no word, just brings her hand across her forehead, arm dropping carelessly at gesture's end.

She frowns. 'You have cobwebs.'

'Well it has been a while, true.'

'In the corners of your room, is what I meant.'

'I know what you meant.'

'I know you know.'

She laughs and closes her eyes. I bring my hand up over her small pot of a belly—in her navel, sweat pools and I sit the tip of a finger inside it, enjoying the faint suction. I lie back on the timber, warmed by spring sunshine coming in through open door and window. My back feels both pained and liberated from recent contortions, arse pressed flat against the grain, manhood lying upon my thigh, defeated. I bring my finger to my lips and taste the sweat of her. It is saltwater.

'Why were you at the forest feast?'

'Mm?'

'You live with the lady. Or did before you toppled her. She lives in a big house far away. So why did you come?'

Now it is Betty up on an elbow, both breasts falling in the one direction again.

'There was a man I liked. He had a dog. The dog bit the lady. He went to prison.'

'The prison on the hill?'

'That one. One day I told my mistress I must travel to a

94

market. It was a lie. A friend of that man took me in his wagon up the prison hill instead, along the cut road, through the wasteland that surrounds the place. I went to the prison gates and asked to see him—the man with the dog. Or the memory of a dog—it's beaten dead now. They said I could only enter if I gave the name of my employer. I could not risk it. I left. The friend of the man with the dog told me of your occasion—'a strange man who sleeps in a forest and now invites us to meet him'. I went to the feast with his family. You passed me some matches.'

'And then you were gone.'

'But then I heard of you a second time: my lady speaking ill of you.'

'Ha.'

'And then a third time: I recognised you on the jetty when she delivered the chest.'

'I recognised you too.'

'I know it—you with your sly wink. And now a fourth time. Now I have come here.'

I watch her, as she rises in her nakedness, as she pads across the warm floor on small feet, grand grabbable arse tapering down to dainty points.

She stares into my empty kitchen drawer. 'Where are your knives and forks? Your spoons? I see the compartments, but they are empty!'

'I am an animal—I eat with my hands.'

'That is madness.' Her laugh is large and round and rises

up through her. 'You are madness.'

She turns, sudden and determined.

'Enough! I will domesticate you. You are my project.'

'Okay, then.' I smile, surprised to find I have just fallen in love. 'I am your project.'

And, both naked as the day, we begin a life.

# 13

## Isaac and Betty's Garden

We have been working on the garden a month now and it is slowly taking on a form. First it was a rough pattern of intent carved in the dunes. (A raised bed will go here. This spot is sheltered from the wind. Here a small shed full of shelves, for now just a rectangle of floor laid bare for the elements.) Then it was a chaos existing somewhere between Nature's wilderness and Man's decree, satisfying neither. Now it is pleasurably both.

Betty swats the air beside her face, not with aggression, simply an invitation to carry on elsewhere. 'The bees are arriving, Isaac. It's a sign.'

A scarf holds her hair up and her brow is sweated. Her

knees are earthy and her fingernails packed with sandy dirt. There is an attractive messiness about her.

I try to impress her with my knowledge. 'They like blue, yellow and white flowers, so we should plant more of these. No double-petalled ones—they find it tricky reaching the nectar in those.'

'How do you know so much about bees?'

'My family kept hives in the garden. In our home, when a death came, I remember Father would kneel and knock on the hive. Explain the death in a low voice. Serious business.'

She smiles and the sun comes out. 'Telling the bees.'

I nod. 'That was it.'

We sit on the bench, warm shirt-stuck backs against the wall. I pull out my tin—I have taken to rolling a number of cigarettes of a morning, enough to see us through a day. I remove two, light both in my mouth, and present hers. She thanks me with a flick of a smile and together we watch the jetty—school is out, the sun is out, and the children of the town leap out over the ocean, each sun-kissed cannonball braver than the one before.

'Did you ever think you'd die in prison?'

She asks questions that seem plucked from the air, wonders.

'At first, every night. I was not made for that place. No one is of course, but some are shown little else so come to almost expect it. Me, I was raised with civility. So when they put me in there—yes. Yes, I imagined my death many times.'

She smiles.

'There was a moment, one day in my third year inside, when a merciless man named Cohen (he was very calm and had a pack of dogs disguised as men who did his bidding) informed me my death was to arrive that night. Such was his power—he could decide and simply announce the event, before guards and gods and all. Then at midnight your barred door would be unlocked. (Cohen carried a skeleton key on a chain.) A giant of a man with a tattooed crow on his face would grab you by the collar and pull you from your cell. And then the gang would take to you with knives, screams echoing as your life was snuffed out right there in that corridor. And no one would bat an eyelid. Ours was an ecosystem, as every small world is, and its rules understood.

'So I returned to my cell that day and stewed. And then— none would be more surprised than me—I slept. I slept a deep and accepting sleep, absolved of sin, aware that when I woke it would be only to die, and then back to sleep I would fall.

'I woke to find the strangest thing—a chair, set in the middle of my cell, with a hanging rope laid atop it. A prison guard's cruel joke or small mercy, I still do not know. Observing these offerings, I could only manage a little smile.

'Midnight arrived and Cohen and his crow-faced golem and three or four others, knives in hand, ambled down the corridor. Each prisoner who heard them pass said a silent prayer for me and rolled over and went back to sleep. Footsteps stopped at my barred door; the thugs peered in.

'My silhouette must have been just discernible in the

gloom—and I could see it surprised them all. Where most men cowered in some corner of the cell on their night of reck-oning, I stood, in the middle of my bare quarters, keen-eyed and waiting. This angered Cohen and he unlocked the door and quick. Crow Face rolled his shoulders and waited for his cue to violence. The door swung open and it came. He reached for my collar and pulled hard, so strong I was lifted clear off my feet.

'But not out of the cell. The rope (one end was tied to the window bars and the other, hidden beneath my prison coat, was wound thrice round my torso) stung furiously but, halle-lujah, it did not give. And so I was suspended in the air, with a monster's hands pulling me towards death and a hangman's rope, ironically, keeping me from it.

'Cohen swore, grabbed a knife from a lackey and slapped the Crow across the back of his inked head, bidding him move. The monster roughly dropped me back to my feet, wind knocked from me but alive all the same. He backed out the narrow door as Cohen strode past him and, without fanfare, plunged the coarse blade into my stomach.

'And a second time I did not end. The knife found itself embedded in the seat of a wooden chair, dismantled that after-noon and now firm against my torso, the noose rope holding it in place. It was not the thickest piece of timber and the blade had managed to pass through—already I felt blood on my belly. But life and death lie either side of a small stream in such moments—happily I stood on the preferred bank.

'A man twice frustrated, Cohen stared at his hand as it tried to free the knife now inexplicably stuck. And in this moment of confusion, I grabbed not at him, but past him and pushed the cell door closed with a great clang. The lock snapped into place, and as one the assembled murderers in the corridor acknowledged the key, along with the man—their boss—was now separated from them by bars.

'I slid a chair leg from my sleeve and rammed it through his heart. He was dead.

'Body folded on the ground, barred door firm between us, Cohen's team of five watched me and I them, a silence taut as rope. They would kill me for this, but they also would have killed me despite this and had not succeeded. The guards would hang me for this, but the guards had already given me the noose and it had been employed. And still I lived.

'A man with a key might then have arrived, the door might have been opened, knives raised, my wick snuffed. But the moment was strange—the five saw I had no great motives beyond this one, that I did not wish to rise higher in stature, as one might when toppling a king. I had no further violence in my system. I simply wished to be left alone.

'So, they left. And they left me alone from then on.

'A warden came by a time later and unlocked the door. But he did not beat me—to death or otherwise. He simply told me where to take the body. He did not help—no one did. I picked up each foot and slowly, deliberately, dragged Cohen out of my cell, then down the corridor, then down the stairs (his head a patient metronome), and finally to the door of the infirmary. Here, they let me leave him, presenting me with mop and bucket in exchange.

'Dutifully I returned the way I came, mopping clean the red trail Cohen, or his contents, had left, step by ascending step, along the corridor, through my door to a final thorough unfouling of my cell. And then, I placed the mop and bucket out in the corridor—and locked myself back in.

'The final years of my sentence were peaceful and uneventful. And then one day they let me out.'

I look down at my cigarette and it has burnt out. Betty's is ash now, dust.

She watches me. She nods. 'So two killers sit side by side on the one bench.'

There is nothing more to say. We are silent. Staring out to sea as bodies tumble through the air and break the surface over and over and over.

# 14

## The Chest

It was a local dive team who went down to do the work. They knew those waters better than anyone, knew the stories that swirled in those waters settling like sediment. And, truth be told, that's all they thought they were kicking up. The tale of the Forest Feast and the Widow's Offer had been around so long it was almost a hymn. Its images filtered the sunlight in the church stained-glass window, adorned in simple carica-ture the coasters that sat beneath every pint at Barbara's. The story had entered into the local sayings. (*An unopened chest is best. See a key, leave it be.*) The site was pointed out to visitors standing at the jetty's end, staring at the breathing water. (*You know what's under there?*) Its key still hung there, all these years later, a century and a half later, on a chain affixed to a hook attached to the bench on the end of the jetty. Rusted away to nearly nothing but still there, tapping on the white wood in the sea breeze, a key in thought not function.

Of course many had tried to find the treasure over the years, gulping in an earthly breath, then launching from the jetty and scrambling down, digging at sand with desperate fingers, both buoyed and sunk by dreams of wealth, until cheeks bulging they rose again.

After oxygen tanks were invented, the efforts grew more considered, the digging was a little deeper. But locals soon put a stop to this—a myth holds its value in the not knowing. If the god you prayed to came down to sit with you one evening, then some of its shine would surely dull.

So it was with the widow's chest. The sense of the town, and what it was, and more importantly what it told itself it was, was shaped by a notion—a dream of how it began and the decisions made, and the way those decisions trickled into whatever came next. So if ever a determined someone plodded flipper-footed to the end of the jetty, with a tank of oxygen and a small spade, the locals would humour them for a few minutes maybe, but then get a kid nearby to jump in and tap the diver's shoulder: 'That's enough now.'

It's a sobering thing to be told polite truths by a child, and most needed telling only once. Chastened, they ascended and waddled back up the jetty.

But next week was one hundred and fifty years since those

first long tables were set in the forest, and everyone wanted some pageantry to mark the day—nothing too ostentatious because this was a modest town. Just a symbol, to set the scene. And of course there was only one.

Niall Mulholland (grandson many greats over of Seb Mulholland who once talked of a town with Isaac) wheeled a good amount of equipment down to jetty's end, assisted by a team of three, all wetsuited and sleek as seals. Two descended (rung by rusty rung, their jumping days long passed) into the cold ocean, and two more lowered down the various tools of the day. The gadgetry beeped and spouted numbers and weights and predictions, and the clever, quiet four of the dive team talked earnestly to each other, then nodded and chose a spot.

It was off a little from where all others had previously set their frantic, breath-held searches. Even with a thing that heavy, the tide had set its table as it pleased. And the chest was deep, astoundingly deep. A hundred and fifty years of ebb and flow sending it down and down and down, burying the treasure, holding the myth interred and intact.

Finally, a digging tool hit something solid and a diver rose and offered a thumbs-up. Those gathered above looked at one another. Was this really happening?

Chains were dropped into the strangely still sea, and attached, and hauled at. A chest awoken from slumber puffed a great cloud of liberated sand into the murk, and rose through the water. Breaking the surface, it gasped at meeting air after so many years and glinted in the sun. It was hauled with the laboured strains of many and banged against the jetty pylons, and worked up and around the precipice. And there, on the end of the jetty, it came to rest.

The chest sat in the spot where, long ago, it was set between two stubborn foes. The metal clasps and brackets were oxidised orange, the fine black wood now a sickly green—but its shape remained. This clenched fist had not relaxed one muscle, and it dared those gathered to reveal its secrets, refusing to help them by collapsing of its own accord. The key, its lifelong companion—separated for so great a span of time by just a few metres of altitude—stared down at it from the bench. But a reunion would not be possible.

So it was a crowbar, indelicate and effective, that did the deed. Wedged behind a buckle, tapped in with a mallet, jemmied quick and sure. The crowd smelled riches and leant in. And then stood back.

It is a child, Lotte Willis, peeking through a forest of legs, who gives the moment words. 'What are they?' And of course she knows what they are—everyone assembled does—but their oddity, in this location, renders them as alien as moondust.

The forks and knives and spoons—tarnished and fused, sat in stasis for so very long—squint into the sunlight. Below them two large stones, added for heft, sit stoic. But it is forks and knives and spoons that take up most of the chest.

'Why cutlery?' asks someone.

Secrets revealed, the chest sighs and collapses in four

splintered directions at once. The key finds a breeze, and
dances laughing on its chain.

∞

Betty rolls away from me and looks at the ceiling.

'I never would have guessed it, Isaac.'

'That was the idea.'

'So when did you make the switch?'

'The first night, after she left in her buggy. I carried to the
jetty two stones from my garden to mimic the weight, and the
cutlery from my drawer to mimic the jangle of coins. Carried
the widow's gold back up.'

'But, what if one of the townspeople called the bluff? What
if someone opened it?'

'No one ever did.'

'But what if they had?'

'Then I would have had to answer that question.'

My answer irks Betty, as I knew it would, as I like that
it did. My feet are hot so I move them outside the blanket.
She leans on an elbow, looking down at me, almost angry. It is
amusing. 'Are you annoyed?' I ask.

'No! I'm not sure. No. So where are they? All the coins?'

'In an old bag. In a place for later.'

'When later?'

'Whenever they are needed.'

Nothing I am saying satisfies her, and I like it—I like the

way her forehead creases. She lies down on her back again.

'It's unbelievable.'

'Wonderful. I truly hope no one ever believes it.'

'So that's why the knives and forks and spoons are missing.'

'Yes.'

'You don't really eat with your hands.'

'No.'

'It's unbelievable.'

'You said that.'

Betty considers what to say next, stretching her arms high, splaying her fingers and staring at them. I think of the seventh-century monk Bede. How he wrote of a system of counting which went up to 9999 simply using the digits of two hands. I think of why we call numbers digits.

'So is it a lot of wealth?'

'It is a very great sum.'

'Could we buy anything?'

'Almost whatever we want.'

'What do you want?'

'That is an excellent question.'

And I raise my arms also, my right hand finding her left, fingers entwined high in the air above us. And our arms become a hill. And our hands are a pinnacle. And lying sleepily in bed, we imagine every contour of the world that we might travel.

∞

At the end of our days, when Betty is old and I am older, we sit on the white bench at the end of the jetty for hours and already, though I don't mention it, I am beginning to recognise the island, to hear the birds. A young couple promenading give us a little smile, the way one does to old people to impress oneself or a girl on your arm. We smile back and they walk away, leaning in and saying small things that make each other laugh. We chuckle at this.

Betty reaches between us and taps the rusting key, so many years old now, sending it swinging. A metronome, but only for a second before inertia wins.

'We never used the treasure.'

'No. We did not.'

'And you never told me where it is buried.'

'You never asked.'

'It is buried beneath the shed, Isaac.'

'Well.' I think quickly about something clever to say. 'Well.'

'You were setting the shed's foundations when I first visited you. And then the shed itself you didn't bother to build for a year. Just the floor. Just at that time. Men are wonderfully obvious.'

She can see my annoyance. It is her favourite game—a shared one.

I look at her concerned. 'Do you mind, Betty? That we did nothing with it?'

'We did things.'

'But grand things. Opulent things.'

'We made patterns.' She rolls a cigarette. 'We live beside the sea and we made a life that is like the sea. We breathed in, and we breathed out. A million times. Others breathed with us. We all breathed together.'

I nod. She lights two cigarettes and passes me mine.

'And we made Constance. And she made Nella. They breathe as well. Maybe the coins are theirs to find. Or another soul's, even later on. Maybe that is the point of them.'

I nod again, and feel my feathers growing, and worry for Betty, and hope she will be okay then, once I start to climb.

It is as if she knows my thoughts, and her head leans softly against my shoulder. And for the first time, I feel her feathers also.

As though to make her point, she takes a deep breath in. And then a deep breath out. And with the next, I join her. And for the one after that too. And on and on and on.

We are two old people, sitting on a bench, the light fading, simply breathing.

# PART THREE

# TILLING

# 15

## The Soldier

When he woke up and opened his eyes, nothing changed.

Or maybe the palest idea of a change was there, a slight sense of light in his vision. But as he thought about it (not with fear—he hadn't got to fear yet), he reasoned maybe this was just heat he was noticing. A strange synesthesia in which his brain read the sun's warmth as a yellow colour because it was landing on his eyeballs. Then the fear. He arrived at fear. His hands clawed at the bedsheets and he discovered he was shackled.

Somebody strong came—firm hands but a soft voice, the dual talents of a capable nurse. She told him he was okay.

He was not okay. He tried to scream this at her but he felt

the recognisable prick in the arm and then his words were water eddying down a plughole, and then just one long word, then just a sound, something indistinct like an animal's bellow. Then nothing.

He woke up again, a year later or a minute, and remembered a little this time. He opened his eyelids slowly now. Vague smudges of perspective, the objects closer to him more distinct, those further away still foggy. Whether they were bedframes or pot-plants or people or lampposts he had no idea. But he was heading in the right direction at least—from chaos towards order. Madness to sanity. He felt too tired to fight, to try to make sense of things, to endure another needle, or strain against the cuffs, so he submitted himself to the dream, and slept.

A third awakening, and this time to a face. The edges more pale, the sockets darker, mouth moving as it speaks.

'Nod if you can hear me.'

Nod.

'Well done.'

Such a patronising statement—he suddenly worries he has been turned into an imbecile. He wants to feel his skull then, to discover if half his brain has been blown away.

'Why are...? I can move my hands. I *can't* move my hands, I mean.'

'I'm a nurse. We are looking after you.'

'Am a prisoner? Am I a prisoner?'

'Not at all. You're safe. You were found beside a road. You

nearly died. Lots of other soldiers did. You're lucky.'

'I don't feel lucky.'

'I know. Here.'

The clicking of metal on metal as the shackles are released. Freedom. His hands rise slowly, scared of what they will reach, or will not reach. He feels his head, all around it with frozen curved hands (just paws for now—no subtlety in the fingers yet). All of his head is there.

'I need to sleep.'

'That's good. You're safe. Sleep.'

He does.

Sitting up, eyes working as eyes again, he can see out the window. There is the sea. He doesn't know which one though—all of them look the same. Are the same, really. Waves just get sent off in different directions, get given shape by different coastlines, but the sea is always the sea. He doesn't recognise this one.

Reaching out into the water is a jetty. It stretches out from a town. Many coloured roofs, a river, a main street, orchards. Then fields. A patchwork. It looks nice. It looks like it raises good people—he trusts its citizens, whoever they might be.

And then a forest. Treetops. Nests. Birds. Just black specks—his eyes are not so good yet. But he loves his eyes. He was so scared of losing them.

The forest climbs towards him, towards wherever this is. Then dead slopes rise up the hill. Nothing grows around this hospital. He is being kept in a place where nothing grows.

He feels tired at this thought. Sleep comes so quickly.

∞

He dreams of the truck: canvas-topped, forlorn men sitting side by side on the benches, rocked violently as the tyres found every pothole. He was drunk, just as he was always drunk in that war. It demanded it of him. Sober, he would have shot every man in sight, pulled the pin on the grenade on his belt and gritted his teeth. Drunk, he could make his way through that war.

They dug up potatoes from any bit of farmland that hadn't been scorched to hell. When they rested in the evenings, those who had survived the bloody day boiled the sad vegetables down to nothing, added barley, a little yeast from a cherished mother, made a mash, and then carried the crude potion in large glass bottles in their bags for as long as possible. Every day he was not shot was another day's fermentation. And when a friend did die, all quietly prayed he would fall face down or on his side, so the bottles he carried wouldn't smash. They closed his eyes, said some words, then unknotted the bag straps from his dead arms and carried the evolving alcohol on to the next place. The next field, the next furrow, whatever it was.

The task motivated them all—keeping those bottles alive was more valuable than surviving themselves. Each bag had a date scrawled upon it and when that date came, those bottles were ready. And the men would get sickly, soullessly drunk.

Drunk enough to swim in a lake in the back of their eyelids. Drunk enough to leave the war and leave the ground and leave everything. Floating—not in a better place or a worse place, but in no place. And then emptied, that bottle was filled again. If they timed everything well, if not too many bottles died on the backs of too many dying men, they could stay drunk all war. They could never know the war existed, even while they did its bidding.

When he had found himself conscripted one morning (hauled off a factory floor, presented with a uniform, a scrap of paper to sign) he had nodded politely and got dressed. War is a great indignity, and the man accepted his lot well. He went where people sent him, he killed who they wanted killed, and he kept himself drunk enough throughout. He ducked the bullets when they came his way, not from a great need to live, just for the sport of not dying. Somewhere along the way he acquired the nickname Treestump, after the stump he chose to stand upon one morning, overcome by the unhealthy need to sing a slurring song despite a firefight raging all around. Both sides laughed and let him live.

A long time later, three years and the bloodied pulp of a fourth, he was a different being, rough stubble on his chin, innocence a dying figment, eyes bloodshot, eyes full of blood.

On that ill-fated last day they were picked up by a truck, wooden-sided and sorry, that was heading towards a place few survived. The moment his company boarded, fodder as all knew they were, their deaths were mostly guaranteed.

But within half a mile they hit something buried, something was triggered, and the truck turned in the air like a football. It landed on its back and broke a great many necks in that moment. Others died from the fire that engulfed them. Others still from bullets sprayed by a party waiting in ambush (uniforms a little different, otherwise men like them, hopefully drunk as well).

Treestump looked so dead he lived. He did not cower, or make a plan to survive. He just lay unconscious, his state pathetic enough not to warrant a bullet.

He lay there until his own side found him, found a pulse, placed him on a ship and brought him here.

∞

'You need to eat.'

'I need to drink.'

She laughs and her laugh is light. He thought she might chide him, but she has heard so much worse. Deafness, the other quality of a good nurse.

'They said you tried to drink the sterilising fluid.'

'It was just sitting there.'

'I imagine they thought no one could be that desperate.'

'Nice to meet you.'

That laugh again. She is not pretty, but when she laughs it draws her a new face.

'Why drunk?'

'What?'

'Why is that the best way to get through this?'

'The war?'

'The life after it.'

He looks out the window at a town busy with life.

'I committed violences. Others died because of them.'

'Well. War takes away our choices.'

He nods. 'And it leaves us our memories.'

She smiles—a nurse's smile. 'Okay. But not disinfectant. It's too strong.'

His eyes do not leave the window. 'What is this place?'

'Well it was a prison. For a long time. And now it's a hospital. A version of one. Until the war ends, I suppose. Then maybe it will be a prison again.'

'Is that why the hill has been cleared so brutally? Nowhere to hide if you escaped.'

'Maybe things will grow back, now the war has stopped it being a prison.'

'It would take so many years.'

'Maybe the war will be that long.'

She speaks with hope and without hope. He looks away from the window. Looks at her face redrawn again.

She laughs. 'Don't start falling in love with me.'

'I'm trying not to.'

She fills his water cup good-naturedly and goes to the next bed.

∞

He is in civvy clothes they have given him. He wears a hat he likes, lopsided, dug out of a box of things discarded by their owners. He holds a bicycle she has found for him. It was in a storage shed—probably belonged to a prison guard who got conscripted too and left it leaning against some shelves for later. Now is later.

'Thank you.'

'You're welcome.' She inhales the alcohol smell of him. 'Where did you find that?'

'One of the guys is brewing it under his bed.'

'You can't remember who, though.'

'I remember he was injured. And wearing pyjamas.'

The smile is nearly as good as the laugh. 'Okay.'

He climbs onto the seat, a little wobbly but remembering.

'Where will you ride?'

'Down this hill, and to that town.' He stares down at the roofs. 'Do you live in one of those houses?'

'I wouldn't tell you if I did.'

'Sensible. Okay then.'

He doesn't push down on a pedal or lean into the handle-bars. He simply lifts his feet, and the slope of the hill and the surface of the road carry him away.

The man raises his hand, and maybe she waves a goodbye back, but he does not turn to see.

# 16

## The Impossibility

Nella Sands is sitting on the bench outside her house in the dunes, a half-filled jar of coins propping the door open, when her visitor comes. The young woman has large eyes and wears a strange jumper, a metal zip at its front as though she is two halves of a person put together. She moves through the dunes like a local, lifts the gate without causing a squeak like she knows its trick. Then she stands at the bottom of the porch steps, wordless, strange yet strangely familiar, waiting to be invited up.

Now both inside, Nella sits in a chair. Her great-granddaughter Liz Mackenzie sits in another, and they watch each other across a worn kitchen table. Nella shakes her head in disbelief.

'It doesn't make sense. But I suppose you realise that.'

Liz nods.

'And you don't seem scared by it, so maybe it's a thing you've done before.'

Liz considers the question, looking down at the tabletop and running her hands patiently across its grain as though trying to understand it. She seems to be someone who is always trying to understand things. She seems tired by this.

'I've been to lots of places. I've been on a boat with a woman who was sailing forever.

'I've been in a fire.

'I've been to the end of my life and seen myself lying in water.'

Liz says these things as if they are normal. As if the facts aren't the problem, only the understanding of them.

Not Nella though. When she doesn't understand a thing—which is often, plenty more often than folk realise—she simply lets it sit a little longer. A teabag left to steep will reveal more of its flavour. But this girl doesn't need a garden walk. Or a lie-down. She just needs to be listened to across a table. She just needs looking in the eye.

'What's your father's name?' asks Nella.

'Andrew.'

'And his father?'

'Toby. Tobias.'

'And his father? You know his name?'

'Treestump.'

'That's not a name.'

'It's a nickname I guess. He and you will make all of us who come after.'

Nella laughs. "Cept I don't know any Tree Stumps—any walking-round ones.'

'Not yet you don't. Later you will.'

'And—I can't make any kids.'

Nella watches the girl shrug and fiddle with that odd zip, like a metal train-track running top to bottom.

A wagtail lands on the windowsill, a bird visiting from the forest nests at the back of the town. It watches them sideways, as a bird does. It turns its head one way then another, getting a bead on Nella and then Liz and then back again. It cannot see both at the same time.

'So are you a ghost then?'

Liz shakes her head. 'Ghosts are from the past.'

A nod. 'That's true.'

'I'm just someone visiting. I turn up somewhere and work out where I am.' She feels the tabletop again, smooth hands on rough wood. 'And then the place makes sense to me. And after a while I leave.'

'So make it make sense to me,' says Nella Sands.

She says this with the love of a great-grandmother. She sees the broiling ocean inside the girl, and wishes it calm. She invites Liz to tell herself how to do that.

But Liz shakes her head, an apology to both women sitting at the table.

'I'm here and then I'm not. That's the only logic to it.'

'Okay,' nods Nella. 'Okay then.' She pours two final cups of tea from the pot that sits between them. 'So, does it end with you? I find 'Treestump'. We make. Tobias. He makes—'

'Andrew.'

'Andrew makes you. Are you the full-stop to it all?'

And for the first time, Liz smiles. She is in love.

'I make a girl.'

'You make a girl, that's good then. Her name is...?'

'Her name is Anja. Your great-great-granddaughter.'

Nella considers how best to say it. But then she just says it.

'And is she like you?'

'No.' Liz smiles. 'No, she's wonderful.'

And both women sit back in their chairs, sit back in that thought, and drink to a girl not yet met.

# 17

## The Bookshop

There was a fire while all slept.

It was a windless night and the blaze had caught well and good before the smoke could float over to another house, find a window, and then a bed, and then a nose, and so raise the alarm.

It was the hairdresser's that went up. Electricity was newish to these parts and a cowboy outfit had travelled door to door making promises, delivering regrets. Wires bought cheap and laid wrong hummed and whispered in the dead of night, before sparking into life amid dusty attic wood, until everything was alight. Until a giant pair of scissors hanging off an awning crashed down onto the street, blue flames running up and down the bubbling paintwork.

The town had no fire department to speak of—just well-meaning volunteers from nearby farms who heard the bell and slung cumbersome trousers and jackets over pyjamas and jumped into trucks. They reached the fire station shed, backed out the pump truck, drew up water from the river, and deposited it—in grand useless arcs—over the blaze.

When it was obvious nothing could be done, and that the neighbouring shops were safe, the townsfolk simply stood on the moonlit street, bleary-eyed and sombre, and watched the fire burn itself out.

Someone lay an arm across Hazel's shoulders as her shop collapsed in on itself. 'We're so sorry.'

Pete Mulholland, who wore the title of Fire Chief as best he could, and the three men and one woman of his brigade hung their sleep-mussed heads. Hazel placed a hand on his arm, all forgiven.

The salon bins had not been emptied and for some days the smell of burnt hair blanketed the town.

Next morning, everyone gathered in the hall, and Hazel sat on stage alongside Jude, who ran things, and the six or seven from the committee. *Happy Birthday Shauna!* said the lopsided bunting behind them, not yet taken down from the twenty-first on the weekend.

Jude spoke first, of heavy hearts and open arms, and Hazel nodded gratefully. Every person there sported one of her cuts, except the ones from the organic farm and Silas who had always got his wife to do his.

Then the hairdresser herself stood, and said she would take it as a sign—and that she and Louise were setting off on their boat and no ifs or buts about it, Lou rubbing Hazel's back supportively all the while. The gathering was shocked as one, but Hazel shushed them and called quiet Michelle up. Michelle stood onstage awkwardly, hands smoothing out the front of a skirt, as her boss declared her no longer an apprentice and fit to take up the scissors herself now—said she just needed a small room with a mirror and a chair for the time being, and Barbara said she had a room as she'd just moved the pool table into the main bar.

So that just left the burnt-out lot on Main Street, and, as with all things in the town, it was a nice loud discussion had that day, with some thoughts challenged but all voices heard. In the end, Alistair's dream of a bookshop was the cream that rose to the top.

Truth be told, no one had ever thought of a bookshop as a business they particularly needed. And Al was newer than most with only fifteen years of parking his bike on Main Street, of batting fourth on the cricket team. But on his arm was Nella Sands, granddaughter of the founder himself—and if Jude ran the meetings, Nella ran the town. No one could name the role she played exactly, just like no one can name the number of breaths they take in a day—they simply take them, and thank god for that.

And Nella had found Alistair, and he her, that day he rode his bike, drunk, into town. And they had brought into the world Tobias who seemed made of sunshine the way he cast a glow, and Maxwell who hadn't come into himself yet but would soon enough, everyone was sure of it.

Alistair stepped modestly onto the stage, weathered old hat in weathered old hand, and explained how in meeting Nella, he'd met her shed too. How it held practical volumes—on shaping timber and raising livestock—decades old and once owned, folks said, by the Founder himself. How Alistair had taken a shine to those books, and so acquired a taste for more. How, in the years since, he'd filled that shed, riding over hills, stopping at distant bookshops, reading dustjackets and wobbling home, bicycle basket full. And it was a sight every soul in that hall knew well, yet another familiarity that made a local feel local just seeing it.

A few folk proposed the rebuilding of the shop. But then Nella said seeing as the shed that held the books held them well, then what say all hands simply clear the fire site, and then a good amount of horses and ropes and strong folk hoist that shed up onto the biggest truck in town (it'd be McGinley's, of course) and head out the driveway that wound through the dunes, and turn left along the Coast Road and turn right into Main Street, and deposit the shed, books and all, in Hazel's old spot?

And it was such a well-shaped Nella kind of answer, a plum answer, that everyone shrugged: 'Of course—of course that'll be the way of things.'

The thick ropes pull taut and the machinery groans. Horses strain, hooves digging into sand as farmers drive them step by desperate step forward, white spit foaming at their bits. The ropes run high, pass over a cantilevered frame (two trunks hammered into the earth, a crossbar between them) and then descend to the shed, to large hooks drilled into the floor joists.

Slowly, creaking its protests, the shed lifts off the earth eighty years after first settling there. It hangs suspended for a magical second, Nella and the kids watching open-mouthed. Then Alistair and the farmers guide it sideways and with a triumphant *doof*, it lands on the long wide bed of McGinley's truck.

The farmers (paid up and hands shook) pat the sweated necks of their beloved horses and untie their ropes.

The frame is lowered and broken down and the truck drives away, McGinley waving his hat out the window of his beast of a machine, proudest man in a thousand miles. Max and Toby run along the driveway after it, jumping onto the back beside their dad, Al's hands pulling them aboard.

Nella watches her garden shed and her three men head up the Coast Road, swinging their legs and talking excitedly.

The noise of trucks and kids and horses and effort fades to nothing. Nella stands in her garden, the day warm and still, the large bare rectangle of dirt suddenly marring a corner of her plot. She goes over to inspect it, wondering whether to plant a bed of vegetables, or seed it more wild, or play no part at all and just let the dunes slowly take it back—the sand has appetite for anything if not kept in check.

Kicking around the granular earth, Nella sees something unexpected. She bends down and loops a finger under it—a bit of leather strapping. She pulls and the earth breaks as the strap is freed in a long furrow, opening up the soil as it goes. Not just a strap but a strap attached to something. She digs a bit, kicks with her toe a bit, gives a bit more heft and loosens it—it is a worn canvas bag, long buried. An Aladdin's lamp, but twenty times the weight. She pulls at it, keeps digging, a farm beast driven by no one but herself.

Success. She frees it and stands back to look at it, as is her way. Maybe she could divine its secrets like she does her humans. But Nella has earned her reputation not by making things complicated—this is a bag. A bag can be opened. She opens it.

She closes it. Her head swims with its contents, and now she is a chess grandmaster mapping a hundred moves in any direction, finding flaws and victories both. What they could do. What the boys could become. Where she and Al could roam. What prosperities the town might know. What horrors.

Nella sits back in the dirt and stares at the coins that offer no explanation, that are so much more inscrutable than a human.

And Nella knows she could wait for Al to get home. For the boys to run in the door. For the town to come sit with her in the townhall or at the end of the jetty and debate what to do with her find. She knows this. But she knows herself too. Trusts herself, her judgment.

She rises from the dirt, slaps her dress clean and goes inside. She walks to Alistair's desk, opens the ink pot, dips the nib in and writes seven words on a slip of paper.

She neatens the desk and folds the paper and walks out onto the porch.

Tools lie scattered and she takes up a hammer and prises four boards loose. She sets them aside and, in the recess, lowers a spade and scrapes aside the coins which landed there so long ago, when Al on his bicycle first came calling.

Now Nella breaks the earth, not too much, just enough. She drags the bag across the garden and up the porch steps. She goes to lower it into the hole created, then remembers at the last minute, pulls the note from her apron and puts it in the bag too.

Then the job in reverse—heap the earth back over the bag, strew those first loose coins upon the earth, put the boards back in place, hammer the nails into them, set the bench above it all. Toss the tools as haphazardly as they were, flatten the earth in the shed's footprint, stamp away the line in the grass that the dragged weight has left, slap her dress clean, stomp up the steps, blow a loose hair out of her eyes, and roll a cigarette.

Sit on your bench. Smoke the cigarette. Savour your home. Wait for your family to come home. Wait to hear their stories. Wait to laugh with them, to run a bath, eat a meal, tuck in your boys, kiss your husband, blow out a candle, breathe out the day, greet the next. And to know. Simply to know.

Great wealth lies here if you want it. Great wealth is not great wealth if you don't want it.

∞

So, three days later, Main Street had a bookshop.

Alistair cut out the front wall beside the door and put a big old window in that the church was tossing, seeing it had a new stained-glass one coming that depicted the Founding Feast—the forest supper. Over a few days, with Max and Toby lugging stock and climbing stepladders, Al had it good to go. And then on a Tuesday (open Tuesday to Sunday, closed Monday) he turned the sign to 'open'.

And everyone came in and bought a first book, some going by a name they knew, some by a cover that spoke well to them, some just by the feel of the thing in their hand. The whole town read then and for a few days after—you saw them sitting on benches, or in the apple barges, or at the bar. And the next week a good many people came back for a second book. And another bunch a little while after that. And a final few decided that one book was their reading adventure done for a lifetime, and turned their mind to other things, fair play to them.

Alistair sat in the shop, the boys sat with him, and Nella came by for lunch and then returned to walk home with them each afternoon. She sat waiting on the step at four o'clock when he'd turn the sign and step out into the sunshine or rainshine or murk, smiling a greeting to her.

They walked slowly down to the jetty, always slowly. Sometimes with the boys running ahead, sometimes just the two of them, mittens in winter, shorts in spring. Sometimes they paused by the river, other times they went straight to the white-salted bench, with the same old relic of a key hanging there on a chain.

As they sat, they talked—about printed fictions he'd just read or human facts she'd just coaxed out, about the friends they shared their lives with, the seasons changing, the sons they were raising, the meals they looked forward to, the grand world turning, the small moments passing.

The boys grew beards and moved away for jobs. Nella's hair grew white. Alistair's grew absent. The shop hours were gradually reduced, and the couple spent ever longer afternoons sitting at the jetty's end. Slowly they came to recognise the birds, to know their murmurations. The dip and lean of a flock, the unspoken agreement of a tumble left, a soaring right. All those brains kindred—an infinite number, and at the same time a singularity.

Nella died when she was old. Alistair handed the keys to the shop to a new couple just arrived. At which point he settled on that bench for good, took up a fishing rod and spent his final patient months casting out into the ocean, reeling in whatever was left, the birds watching on.

He was buried in the forest, beside Nella.

# 18

## Conor the Free

The home was a care facility, not a prison (even if the dynamics inside made it hard to tell the two apart sometimes). So that meant you were in there until you were old enough to live alone or lucky enough to live with someone else. But it still let you access the outside world, as long as it was for a sensible reason (like training for a job) and not another kind (like wandering in a forest spied through a window to seek out birds who felt like parents). And maybe given the chance I could have argued what *sensible* really meant—how if they wanted to raise good humans, then forests might be better places to learn in than factories. But I wasn't given the chance. So Tuesdays to Fridays, those of us who were fifteen or older went down to the town and learnt skills.

Mr Richards took us in a bus and it wasn't like school where the hard kids sit up the back, because we were all hard kids, so everyone just sat everywhere. Some kids slept, some studied their resumés and practised speaking the words, and some just stared out the window—at the bare hill, then the warm woods, the fields laid out, and the sea beyond it all.

They were savouring the experience of liberation, of course, but for me it never really worked, even with all the chapel hours I put in trying. In the end, you were still looking out through glass—still in a place not of your choosing. And you could set me up at a window looking over Niagara Falls or the pyramids or all the way out into space, and I'd still feel set up. We don't all think the same though, which is good.

Pat loved staring out and would mention things he saw in the distance, places he'd visit with his mum one day. And I think that on those mornings he could pretend he was just a guy on a bus going to work. Doing a thing to make money to feed his family. Not in love with his job but in love with the reason for having it.

Eventually the hill slope levelled out and we passed through the woods, beneath the birds and their nests. And then the forked roads converged and we were on Main Street. And I'd be looking out the window too, not to notice every normal thing, but just one special thing. Liz was never there though—sitting on a bench, or waiting for a bus, or idling in a car writing a poem. Maybe she had left the town already. Or maybe she was bunkered down deep in its belly—waiting for everyone to stop worrying and become calm. Or waiting for night to come. Or waiting for me.

Pat got dropped off first, and then a guy called A (just A— we never found out the full thing) at a garage because he was good with cars. And then a couple went to the general store because they didn't know what they were good at. And then me, at Maggie and Haytham's shop.

Haytham's from the Middle East and bald and Maggie's Irish and round. And back then the two of them ran a small bookshop on the main street of that town. It was a funny place for a Qatari man and an Irish woman to end up, but it was a funniness that fit. If you were new to that town and met Haytham and Maggie while wandering the streets of that town, they'd hold your attention a little longer than another thing.

But if you were a local that wasn't the case—except maybe on some drunk night at a bar when someone on the stool beside Haytham would lean in and ask a question the sound of which was ignorance, but the intent of which was learning. And of course Haytham would humour that question and answer as best he could, because mostly between friends it's not the taste of the pie but the fact you bothered to bake it.

The pair drove an old sedan to book markets on weekends. They were canny with tracing ISBNs and could pick rare finds and naïve people. They weren't shady in their dealings. But they weren't made of solid gold either.

They'd travelled a great deal and much of the shop was a nod to the grand wide world and its people and oceans and flimsy changing borders. Sometimes they'd take fiction and shelve it geographically, *The Sun Also Rises* in the Spanish section, *Invisible Cities* in Italy, invented stories slid between real ones. It was nice how they did that because it made everything feel equivalent. Not in the trite notion, that history is made up. But in the nicer one, that fiction is at its heart true.

And it wasn't like the ones at the home decided a small unconventionally run bookshop that barely made money was the right fit for a quiet sixteen-year-old with abandonment issues. There was no kindly teacher who saw potential in me before I could: maybe finding me graffitiing a toilet door and going to clip my ear, but then remembering a time when she was young and might have been more than she was. That wasn't a thing that happened.

What did happen was I got set up with a regular six-hour shift at Benji's, a bad chicken place run by a stooped woman named Gillian. The Benji in question had run out on her years before, but Gillian still walked into work right under his name each day. Which I think was the cause of her stoop—always having to duck your head as you pass under a failed love would do that to you.

The misery hung off Gillian, like the cooking sweat that congealed on the kitchen walls until the heat rose high enough and gravity sent it south, travelling grouted canals between once-white tiles. Misery makes some people loud, but it made

Gillian quiet, and she'd sit long hours in an uncomfortable plastic chair smoking Lucky Strikes in those days when tobacco and food prep weren't separate things.

She was never busy, but any time you asked a question she'd miss it. When you asked a second time, she'd bat the air with a weak hand and stare at you, like the smoke around her was a heavy curtain and only now could you be seen.

'The mop, Gillian. Have you seen it?'

And she'd think (slowly). And look back at you (slowly). And point a sad, wedding-ringless hand in its direction. Or if more detail was required she'd sigh, and then speak some words, the smallest number she could. And then sigh again and light another smoke.

In the meantime, I cleaned the surfaces and served the customers and cracked jokes with Juana the chicken cook. She had cauliflower ears from a dad who beat her, and a photo of an awkward-looking man stuck up over the sink, and a wicked sense of humour that would've got her fired if Gillian ever worked up the energy to hear her. Except it wasn't just that Gillian took no notice—Juana had a pair of innocent eyes that meant she could call you the filthiest name right to your face, and you'd get mad at yourself for imagining a vulgar thing. She once confessed to me she stabbed a girl in a cinema carpark when she was my age—but with those eyes of hers I couldn't bring myself to believe it. Juana carried guilt, the kind that comes with wanting to own up to a wrong but having a face that won't let you.

The few months I worked at Benji's threatened to undo every minute of forest-looking I ever clocked up, and almost set me low enough to stay working there for the rest of my life. The only redemption was offered up by geography: the fact that beside the chicken shop stood a laundromat.

And beside the laundromat, a bookshop.

I took my smoke breaks in the carpark out the back, even though Gillian wouldn't have cared if I lit up right beside her. Even with the stinking bags of bones and grey chicken flesh, cooked a second time in the sunlit dumpsters, that had everyone praying all week for Fridays when the bin men came.

Smoking wasn't even a thing I did back at the home but at Benji's I smoked to stay healthy. Without a cigarette to explain myself, Gillian would never have let me outside for five minutes in the hour. But by digging through a pouch and rolling something clumsy, holding it up with a questioning eyebrow, I'd get the shrug of permission and be out the door. Then, in a zipped jacket, I'd stand in the carpark's furthest corner from the bins for a few moments free of the misery inside the shop.

It was a Tuesday, maybe my third smoke break, when a bald brown guy backed out of the bookshop with a heap of flattened cardboard for recycling. When he saw me, he stopped for a second, then finished the job, calling out as he returned, 'You at the chicken place now?'

It was weird, how the face and accent said somewhere else, but the sentence itself—short, familiar, right words missing in the right places—said local.

I'd learnt long ago that conversation meant trust, and trust meant trouble, so I pointed at my apron with an unimpressed finger, asking without asking: what did he think?

'And what—you working at my bookshop as well are you?' he continued.

I scoffed and muttered loud enough he could hear. 'No chance.'

'Right,' he nodded. 'Then stop leaning against my fucking car.'

And before I could shout something back, he was inside and the screen door slammed shut.

Because I was proud, I didn't go and investigate the bookshop that Wednesday. Because I was less proud than I thought I was, I went on the Thursday.

'All out,' I shrugged to Gillian, waving an empty tobacco pouch through the opaque chicken-shop air. 'Need anything?'

And Gillian considered her needs then, considered the avalanche of wrongs in need of righting for her to be remotely happy again, and mumbled for a Snickers. Nodding, I headed out the front door instead of out the back.

It was late autumn and Main Street carried a draught all the way along it. The trees were bare, bracing themselves against the cold, and the few people dotted around wore raised collars and low beanies, just a small sliver of face remaining. I zipped my jacket to my chin and turned left for the tobacconist. I bought my regular pouch and a Snickers and returned to the street for the quick journey back.

But of course I didn't go back. I slowed my steps, and planted my feet at the thin shop frontage that was mostly given to a shelf-filled window, begrudgingly shared with a small recessed door—as if the books were a pleasure and the customers an afterthought. Looking through the glass at spines wedged into shelves, I saw a couple of familiar names and a whole lot more unknown—books hadn't been a part of my last years.

Turning the icy doorknob, I entered.

∞

After I'd looked for as long as possible without committing, I prised one off the shelf and lay it on the counter in front of Maggie (who I didn't yet know was Maggie). Feeling more scared than I'd ever been in the home, I nodded a small nod at the book and smiled a small smile at the woman.

'That's a great one,' she said.

'Oh. Good,' was my nothing reply.

'He wrote some nice stories a while back. And then two terrible ones in a row, so everyone gave up on him. But this is the next thing he did—his best thing.' She laughed. 'Only no one cares any more. You know him, do you?'

I shook my head. 'I just like that it's about a ghost train.'

She nodded and put it through the till.

'Well, fair play for not pretending.'

She gave me my change, smiling conspiratorially. 'I like that it's about a ghost train too.'

And the coins handed back to me were already warm from that small moment she'd held them. And the exchange left me feeling better (exactly the opposite of any chat with Gillian). And the carpet felt thick beneath my feet, the shelves felt strong and sure and full. And the song that played was in that moment one I desperately wanted to hear all the way to its end, and I regretted choosing my book too quickly and denying myself more time in there. But I made to leave, forcing myself to return to cold winds and warm chicken fat and muted bus ride back to the room that wasn't a cell but that wasn't not one either.

'Carpark boy,' said the man, entering from the backroom with two cups of tea and giving one to Maggie. 'What'd he choose?'

I stood at the door and held it up.

'Did you recommend it?' he asked Maggie.

'Nothing to do with me. He likes the ghost train idea.'

'But the train is just a metaphor.'

'Yeah. He likes that too.'

And I could have just kept standing there awkwardly, but I gave a small wave and left. I walked the two doors back to Gillian's. Then I hung up my jacket and tied on my apron and read that book for the rest of the morning. When the lunchtime rush came, I set it aside for a bit, and then later I had to wipe down the countertops and mop the floors and take out the greasy chicken bags. But any minute I could, I read the book. And on the bus back to the home I read the book. And that night I finished the book, and put it on my shelf. Then I slept the sleep of someone who's just finished a story, one where half your dreams are there already.

The next day, a Friday, I went back to the bookshop, in the small handful of minutes between the bus leaving and my shift starting. Maggie and Haytham were laughing when I walked in, laughing enough that I checked the 'open' sign on the door, as though humour that honest couldn't exist during business hours. They stopped and looked at me, smiles still on their faces.

'He's finished it already. I knew he would,' said Maggie.

Haytham dropped the smile. 'Like it?'

'A lot,' I said.

'Even though the ghost train was just a metaphor?'

'Except...it wasn't really. The metaphor was so...real it was a thing. Not a clue to another thing. But a thing itself.'

They looked at each other, and nodded, and suddenly I felt in on the joke I'd just missed. As though there'd been all these variables: whether I'd walk in or not, or whether I'd have read the book or not, or whether I'd give an answer or not. And those three correct moves (unplanned, just as they had to be) set in train everything that was to follow.

'You like working at Gillian's?' Haytham asked (and I appreciated how he used her name and not her husband's).

'Job's a job,' I shrugged.

'Is it so?' asked Maggie. 'And they choose where you work this job that's just a job, the fellas up on the hill there?'

'Yeah. Or I guess so. No one's really said. You just work where they send you. Why?'

And the *why* was just a word, but it was also me being braver than I'd ever been.

'Oh well, business is booming as you can see,' said the Irishwoman, 'and this one and me are off on the road a lot getting new stock. If you're standing round all day leaning on Gillian's counter and Haytham's car, no harm in you leaning on this counter instead. Plus, no disrespect, but I doubt your home on the hill charges the big bucks for your services.'

I shook my head and Haytham slid a pen and paper across the counter.

'Write down the home's number and we'll see if we can sort it.'

And I did, putting *Mr Richards* in brackets beside the number and sliding the paper back to Haytham.

'I'll make the call,' he said, and I nodded and waved and walked out the door.

Only on the street did I realise I'd forgotten to buy another book. Only back at the chicken counter did I realise I'd forgotten to say yes to even wanting the bookshop job. Only at day's end, when Mr Richards shook Gillian's hand, and Gillian shook Haytham's hand, and Haytham shook Mr Richards' hand, and Mr Richards gave me a kind little thumbs-up, did I realise this was real.

I went to apologise to Gillian—but was surprised to find a knowing look in her usually dull eyes. She knew she was losing me that day before I did, knew it the same way she knew every loss that had befallen her. She was a woman people left, and I would like to have proved her wrong. But not enough to stay. My silent excuse just became an echo of the ones before, and I went.

Juana gave me the finger as I walked out the door, and we both laughed.

# 19

## Haytham and Maggie

Haytham came from a rich Qatari family, one that made its money in diplomatic relations—the kind found in that moment when an insular country opens up to a big world and needs people who'll shake many hands and leave little paper.

Haytham was a baby then but a baby blessed and, though he shunned it all once old enough, it was wealth that forged him. So when he grew his hair long and listened to bootleg Joe Cocker records smuggled in by the kids of diplomats and moaned about injustice in the world, the world saw him as the thing he was: a rich man cursed by luck. Try as he might, shouting his vitriol at those who ran things, he could not annoy them. He was one of them—they all saw it. So they pretended to be angry and waited patiently for him to return to the fold.

Realising this, he left Qatar and invited the world to wipe the sheen off him—rich or not, an Arab wandering a white land faces things he must endure. After an adolescence of wishing cops would chase him down streets (instead of whisking him quietly home to his father, muttering apologies), or wishing mothers would warn their daughters about him (instead of bringing them to the house to sip apple tea and smile politely through awkward silences), now he had his fill.

White families crossed the road. Bar staff refused him entry. The police with their funny high hats turned his pockets out whenever the mood took them. Once a group of young men beat him up in the low light of a Tesco's carpark. They weren't even shaven-headed fascists; they were just boys doing a simple dance upon his brown body to impress the girls who leant against a wall, to impress the men who hid inside the boys.

At a point Haytham was so hungry he cried and was wired funds that burnt his hands—the remnants of wealth lingered in knowing he could return at any time and want for nothing. He caught a ferry then, and began hitching around Ireland. He travelled from Mallen Head to Mizzen Head (furthest north to furthest south) in short bursts, the bemused drivers either interrogating this alien in their land or saying not a word and concentrating hard on roads that needed no concentration.

In one town he met a local guy called Joe and the two shared a powdery joint, then stumbled laughing down the high street to an Irish pub, the type poorly imitated the world over. Old men sat on old chairs, a dog kept a place by the fire, paint peeled off the walls, and sawdust covered the floor, to be swept into the hearth at night's end.

The publican, Joe explained, was packing it in after thirty years and, having no sons of any worth, it was falling to his daughter, Maggie. Joe pointed a stoned finger and there she stood, behind the taps, a weary seriousness on her face as she pulled pint after pint.

∞

Haytham stood there—twenty-two years old, lost, tired, old bruises fading into dark skin, old privilege fading into dark poverty, a man shipwrecked. And, not meaning to, he fell in love at first sight.

Maggie was oblivious to this, just as the ones we fall in love with should be. Her cheeks, red at the best of times, burned with the effort of a long shift and the fire's heat. Her breath caused a particularly beautiful indent at the base of her neck to rise and fall, which made the small crucifix she wore there tilt ever so slightly, so gently as to be near invisible, or to make every other thing disappear once it caught your eye. Sweat beaded on her temples. Her hair was tied back and held with a wide clip. Her lips were full.

Haytham sat in awe, watching Maggie work, and as the night went on he became angry. Work was all she did—her father, having pulled a couple of ceremonial pints early in the evening, was now settled on a stool holding court with loud tales, thirty years of barman's secrets let loose as the locals roared with embarrassed laughter. All the while the old man avoided eye contact with his daughter, simply tapping the bar with an empty glass when in need of a full one and uttering no word of thanks when he received it.

The others too barked gruff orders at the poor girl who raced between taps, and rolled kegs, and heaved a log onto the fire when the flame grew weak. Not a kind word was passed her way, even by Joe who got the pints (Haytham having paid for the weed earlier).

*What horror has she inherited?* Haytham longed to ask.

But to be foreign is to be mute, and he knew this.

By midnight the wandering Arab had had enough and was on the verge of doing something—the details were blurry—when the father rose from his stool. He lifted a hand and all were silent. Leaning against the bar to steady himself, he spoke.

'I love this bar 'cause I've grown old in it. And I love all of you 'cause you've grown old in it beside me. And if I had more energy, I'd stay behind the bar there, listening to all your bollocks like every other night. But I don't, so I'll stand this side now and talk some bollocks of me own!'

There was laughter. Then he looked to his daughter.

'And Maggie. Of course it's yours now.'

Haytham waited for this father to say a proud father's words, to describe her greatness, to explain to Haytham the magic she possessed that made men fall in love with her from across a room.

'Maggie, give us a song.'

That was all he said. And though the room was silent before, the silence intensified then. It found its way into every corner, settled on every shoulder, made the wind cease and the fire pause its crackling. Maggie—tired and sweating, watched by every person in the bar—slowly, awkwardly, heaved herself up onto the bar. She grunted and clambered and not one person offered a hand. Finally she stood, smoothing down the front of her dress, sleeves damp with beer. And she closed her eyes.

The song Maggie sang that night, in her father's pub in a small town in County Cork, was her song. It was the song she sang aged eleven, standing shyly in the middle of her lounge room when her ma had friends for tea. It was the song she sang while staring into bonfires, passing a bottle with teenage friends. It was a song for a funeral, or a farewell, or a celebration. And it was the perfect song for that moment when your father decides what's his is now yours. And when your town decides it too.

Without her knowing it, it turned out to also be the song you must sing to a rich man to make him, for the first time in his life, feel truly poor. Now, even if he were to fly straight back to Qatar, Haytham realised—even if he were to inherit every coin, every connection—there would still be an absence.

And yes, maybe once home he could derive some pleasure from remembering her—remembering this night, this moment—just as a guiding star is still seen from far away. But stars are not companions in shipwreck.

Her last note ended, the silence returned and the gazes lingered. Maggie held each one, then lowered herself down from the bar. Taking up her position behind the taps, she stared out at the customers she'd inherited. For as long as a minute, no one moved.

Then an old man stepped out of the throng and slowly crossed the empty space. Placing coins upon the worn wood, he spoke with a respect so quiet it echoed.

'Could I have one pint there, please, Maggie?'

And those words were the window opened in a musty room, permission for every bystander to exhale. And together they rushed the bar and addressed their friend, their publican—laughing, chatting, thanking. Suddenly Maggie had always been there, had never not owned the bar. And her da stood with his friends, just another person in the crowd.

It had taken a song, but it was not the song. It had taken a ritual, but it wasn't the ritual. It was simply a moment, doing what great moments do—assuring us of the present (of our ability to feel a thing now, to be alive now).

This is love, Haytham realised while revelling in his newfound poverty, a boy turned into a man turned into a boy. And, recognising a companion with whom to weather the tempests, to watch the stars, he went up to the bar and ordered a drink.

# 20

## Arrivals

The years tumbled into one another. The Arab and the Irishwoman travelled together, and fell further in love, and fought a bit, and grew a bit. Eventually Maggie tired of her country, just as Haytham had of his, and they found a new one, strange to them both, and made it their own.

In this land the pair travelled. They scoured cities and towns and vast daunting plains, loving some parts, hating others, welcomed, fended off (not with overt acts, just cold politeness). Until the moment, on a stretch of desert road no different from that of a mile back or a mile ahead, when their car stalled. Over the next hours, the sun sang a single high note to them, a shrill ceaseless buzz. That night, sun gave way to a cold moon and they huddled in the backseat, knotted round each other. The plan was to conserve heat but really each pulled warmth from the other until they both froze.

That morning the sun returned fierce and single-minded. It glinted off the windscreen and heated the metal of the chassis, the vinyl of the seats. It made the road ahead dance and wobble—the desert breathing, the air a dream.

Haytham and Maggie sat in the car, still as possible, wordlessly passing a last bottle of warm white wine found in the boot. Silently, they counted time in their heads and mapped a grim equation.

When the patrol car did come by, and the leather-skinned, desert-moulded cops stepped out and tapped on the window, Maggie could manage only a whimper.

∞

'What is this place?'

'Immigration. You're being held here, while we find out who you are.'

'I can tell you who I am.'

'Respectfully, our ways are more effective.'

'Where's Haytham?'

Nothing.

'Where is he?'

'Shouting doesn't make things move faster here.'

Maggie ignores the cold room and the cold man, and stares

out the window. She's up high, on a bare hill holding nothing but herself. There are woods below. Then a town. Then the sea. It doesn't look like the one she knows, the dark Atlantic and its endless waves, white fingernails clawing at the Irish coast. This sea has spent its life warmed by sunshine—it holds no grudges. And wheeling above it, banking and turning on the wind, fly the birds.

∞

'Her name's Maggie. She has red hair. Is she in another room? Is she okay?'

'Where did you begin driving from, and what was your intended destination?'

'I asked you a question. You can't just ask me a question back.'

'We found passports in your luggage, but no visas. Which is odd.'

'It's... I travel diplomatically—I was given permission. And the permission extends to Maggie too. We haven't broken any laws.'

'Did I mention any laws? Any breach of any laws?'

The man is very calm, almost good-natured in that way cruel people can be. Every hour he comes in and asks questions. Every hour he leaves again. He can do this—go in or out of the room. Haytham can't. A bird comes to the window-sill, just there on the other side of the pane, separated from him by nothing and everything. It considers this large brick building here on the barren hill, considers the nests humans make for themselves. Then, bored and restless, it flies to its own. Haytham watches its form dip above the canopy of forest. Beyond, he sees smoke rising from small houses. Beyond that, a jetty.

'What is that place?'

'Show me your visas and you can see it for yourself.'

'I told you. I don't need a vi—'

'But if you want to make things difficult...' The sigh the man gives is not frustration, but sympathy. 'Then I am in no rush. My colleagues are in no rush. We can wait. Maggie can wait.'

'So she is here!'

'Of course.'

The man smiles, gathers up his paperwork, and is gone again.

Haytham goes to shout something, but the words fade before they can reach the departing bureaucrat. He leans his head on the cool glass and watches the world outside, the world beyond this desolate hill.

His heart aches—for Maggie, for freedom. But a hope whispers too. Down there, wherever down there is, intrigues him. Sometimes the worst leads to the best. He knows this. Sometimes a bad thing isn't really a bad thing—we endure a moment now to meet its reason later on.

So, okay, he will be in no rush. He will be quiet and polite and make no fuss. Inside, yes, he will seethe and roar, but on the surface he will answer the questions and bear the silences. He knows Maggie will too—he watched her at the bar that night, knows she understands time and patience and the things one earns.

She might be looking out a window too, down at that place too. Their hope might be the same.

∞

Finally, almost arbitrarily it seemed, Haytham and Maggie were let out into the sunshine. Beyond clanging gates, on a wind-whipped hilltop, they stood and cried and held each other. They were so angry with the months lost and the men responsible that they never mentioned them again. Instead they turned their backs on that place and walked down the hillside.

A forest of dense foliage wrapped itself round the back of the town, a broad shoreline spanned the front, and a salt-crusted jetty stretched out over the waves. But forests and jetties were mere peripheries to their story. In the town's middle was a secondhand bookshop, dying, run by an old man, dying.

Alistair had planned to see out his days sitting at his old counter between his old shelves, stared down upon by his old tomes. But Maggie and Haytham offered too much money and he could not say no. He signed paperwork and handed over keys. Then he walked down Main Street and sat on the jetty with a fishing rod leant lazily beside him, watching the birds that watched the catch. He died some months later, happier than he would've been had life not interrupted.

Maggie and Haytham dusted the books, reordering things as they saw fit, but understanding too how patterns work, how small towns grieve, and leaving much as it was. They filled their days comfortably and their pockets modestly and slowly grew from young blow-ins into old regulars.

One day the childless couple took in a parentless youth from a cruel building that was once a prison, and then a hospital, later an immigration facility, and then a juvenile home. They offered him no polish, few words of life-learned wisdom—just space and a role to play in the town's small ecosystem.

Haytham never inherited his millions. Maggie never passed on her song. But their life was one many people quietly aspired to. And any man who might feel sorry for them was only advertising the fact he still had things to learn about happiness.

# 21

## Conor and Liz's Reunion

I'd been working at the bookshop three months when she came in.

By then I'd found my rhythms, stepping off the bus Tuesdays to Fridays and heading up the laneway to the carpark—the bins of chicken bones still stank but now I could just be another frustrated observer.

At the back of the shop I took out my key, and each time I did a small warmth rose in me—the memory of how, at the end of my first shift, Haytham had mysteriously shrugged on his overcoat, ignored Maggie when she asked where he was going, and headed out the front door into the cold. How ten minutes later he returned and placed that key on the counter in front of me along with a pack of chewing gum.

'Stop smoking,' was all he said, and Maggie smiled to herself.

I pocketed the offerings as casually as possible, fooling no one.

The key couldn't be kept in my dorm because it could be weaponised. So Mr Richards held on to it and each time we headed to town on the bus, he handed it over. At first he'd do this as I stepped off the bus at the shop. But soon he sensed its importance and began giving it to me right at the home gate. I'd turn it over in my hands all the way down the hill, feeling the trust rising off it, as Pat stared out the window and chatted away about nothing.

I'd hang my jacket on one of the hooks, and in the small kitchen alcove I'd make three cups of tea. Maggie loved a strong Irish one called Barrys (she and I had it milky; Haytham took just sugar). Elbowing aside the curtain hanging over the doorway, I'd step through to the bookshop proper. It was always warm, and there was always music, and the two of them were always sitting either side of the counter, finishing off the cryptic crossword. The bus wasn't punctual and I could arrive a few minutes either side of nine, but no matter when I did, they'd be struggling with the final three or four clues. They'd ask, I'd answer, then they'd nod and ink them in, a small repeated pretence we all chose to go along with.

Then Maggie gave me the ledger for Saturday and Sunday (we were closed Mondays) and the pair stocked shelves as I entered last week's takings into a clunky old computer. At 9.30 we gathered round the paper and turned to the nine-letter anagram. Whoever got it first picked the music and once it was playing, I turned the sign to 'open'. Then for seven and a half hours I worked in a bookshop.

Early on Haytham had said, 'Don't think you'll just be sitting round reading all the time.' But I pretty much was. Sure there were customers, and stock needed shelving and sales needed logging and there was dusting and bins to empty and receipts to spike and tea to make and music to change. But the unspoken truth I quickly realised was that Haytham and Maggie had run the shop for years without help, and the only one who really needed the job was me.

But they were getting older, and with me at the counter they could more easily get in the car and hunt out more secondhand volumes. Or get in the car and go home for lunch. Or get in the car and simply drive. And this stepping back was something they well deserved.

∞

Then one Thursday, I'm sitting at the counter reading a thin book by a dead author. The bell tinkles and there she is, a silhouette in the doorway.

'You look lighter.'

Her words are a perfect observation. I do, and I am.

I smile at the niceness of this, and gesture to the shelves

as explanation. Liz nods, like it's enough of an answer, then removes her sunhat (spring has come after a long winter) and walks up to the counter. A small pot of bookmarks in the shape of trees sits near my elbow and she shuffles through them, fingers just centimetres from mine.

'So you're here now? That's good.'

'I'm both places.' I shrug. 'Four days here and the rest up on the hill.'

'Hard, switching between two worlds.' She puts a silver birch and a dollar on the counter.

Nodding, I put her dollar in the till. 'Better than having just one. Hey, I found your poem.'

I stand up from my squeaky stool and walk round the counter. For a moment, as I navigate the small space, my shoulder brushes hers and the joy of this goes unspoken. I walk straight to where the book sits on its shelf, flick to the right page, and hand it to her.

She smiles. 'You practised that.'

My face reddens and I pray she won't look up from the book.

'Strange I haven't seen you,' I say. 'Not in three months.'

'Yeah well, I don't come in when you're working.'

I laugh.

'So you still making worried people worry? Or did you make the switch to calming people?'

Liz raises her eyebrows and points at me, impressed. 'Good memory, smart guy.'

I shrug.

She puts her sunhat down on the counter and flips through the book.

Then she goes and puts it back on the shelf.

'The second one. The calming one.'

'Well, that's good.'

I smile. She doesn't.

'Isn't it?' I say.

Liz nods and then reaches up for the same book again, this time brings it to the counter.

'Yeah. Yeah, it's really good. Just this one, thanks.'

I put it through the till, not sure what just happened. The album suddenly reaches its end, and the silence that arrives is heavy. The shelves lean in on us, taller than they were.

She pockets the change without looking at it, slides the book off the counter, and goes to the front door quickly, a ghost's footsteps on the thick carpet. Giving a wave, which feels like an apology, she is gone before the bell can ring.

Her hat lies forgotten on the counter.

∞

I don't sleep well for the next nights.

But when she comes in a week later, her smile is large, our last strange ending a figment. She stands in the doorway and points an accusatory finger.

'You're the thief from the home who stole my hat!'

An old woman looking at cookbooks eyes me warily for the briefest second, and I give her a friendly smile, then shake my head pleadingly at Liz.

She just laughs a big light laugh and takes the hat off the wall hook where it's been hanging, waiting for her return.

'There you are!' she says and she throws it on and twirls around, chin raised, eyes closed, euphoric.

She looks beautiful, so beautiful my week of worrying is suddenly forgotten.

That was Liz's magic trick, and it worked lots of times before it didn't anymore.

'I just came to give you this.'

She slides the silver birch bookmark across the counter to me, a phone number now written on its trunk.

'Wouldn't your parents hate you seeing a boy from the home?'

She beams. 'Yes!'

And she waves, floating through the shop and out the door, the bell ringing her goodbye, me staring foolishly after her.

'Is this one good?' The cookbook woman rudely holds a book about vegetables in front of my face.

It isn't but I nod and ring it up.

At the end of my shift—the hours had passed both faster and slower than usual—I say bye to Maggie and Haytham and step out into the sunshine.

Liz kisses me straightaway, right on the step of the shop. So I don't go back up the hill. Instead we sit on the salty bench at the end of the jetty, and kiss and talk and talk and kiss. She has one sister and I have nobody. ('You win,' she says.) She used to be good at track but they kicked her off the team because she wouldn't commit. Her lips are cracked and she tastes like salt-and-vinegar chips and her freckles are out. Her eyes seem rounder than most people's—like everything is a wonder to her—and at the end of our hour together she leans her head on my shoulder and we just look out to sea and watch the birds as they tumble through the air and then catch themselves an inch above the waves, shadows on the water.

And even though lots of things with Liz aren't good later on, that moment is perfect. That moment of sitting and leaning, after the words, after the kissing. Just sitting. And I'm not saying that one hour balances out all the shit times after. But I also know it'd be a tricky equation, working out just how much of the sadness I'd put up with to keep it.

Not all the sadness, no. But probably a lot.

∞

I move out of the home soon after, and Liz moves with me. Her family's always had this shack by the water, in among the dunes, where they store stuff for the beach or let people stay when they're visiting. We make it really nice, like a real home. And then we fill it with anger, pollute it. And then we make it feel nice again. It's a little harder each time.

Liz is there, and then she's not. Her sadness sometimes

comes in great big waves that crash against the house. Other times it's a quieter thing—we could be sitting at the big old table, eating, talking. And then her hand will pass across the surface, like she's sweeping away crumbs. And she'll lay her cheek on the wood, and cry into the wood. At first, I used to try to comfort her. Eventually I just set down my fork and waited for her to finish.

And it was strange—grief and loss were languages I spoke, things any orphan understands. Only her loss I couldn't find. It didn't seem to exist behind her, which is where loss usually lives. Or even in front, like the weight of a terminal illness or a sick planet. Liz's seemed to be something made new every moment, a tragedy happening now and now and now. But then flung away in these brilliant, bright moments where she was magical, where she seemed to ripple with life. And then she'd be crying on the table again, me shuffling potatoes round my plate.

Anja is born late in the spring and she nearly dies. She's blue and limp and silent and the nurses are shouting things and people are running (plastic sensible shoes on sterile floors). And then she screams the biggest scream. She roars at all of us, and the doctors and nurses all laugh and hold their chests and mouth the word *phew* to us through kind smiles.

And we stare at each other, the three of us, bewildered, trying to make sense of what happened.

I go back to work at the bookshop and Liz stays in bed. First it's in bed with Anja, so we don't really notice it.

'You'll be tired in the first year,' says everyone.

And it is the first year, so that's what she is.

But then it's the second year. And Anja has had enough of being in bed—she comes to work with me, and goes driving in the country with Haytham and Maggie, all of them blowing raspberries at the cows.

But Liz stays in bed. She burrows down between the sheets and whenever we talk she just tells me about her dreams.

'But dreams aren't anything?' I tell her. 'This is. She is, that girl sitting by your feet and playing with the bottom of your pyjama leg. I am. The town is. The seasons are. Day is. Night is. You're missing all of it.'

She just keeps telling me about her dreams. If I push too hard, she simply smiles and closes her eyes, pretending to sleep.

Haytham and Maggie give me the shop. I mean, they sell it to me for so little it's a gift. They say it's enough. And we all hug. And we cry and laugh. And Anja is there with us, laughing too.

Liz isn't. She'd already taken the car by then, one day a while ago when I was at work and Anja was at school. She drove off in a direction we could probably find out. But we didn't. We didn't try to track her down. We didn't even feel guilty about that. Or sad. Or at least an amount of sad beyond the quantity that had filled our house for a long time. She drove away, and we let her drive away.

I speak with Anja that evening, as we sit on the bench at the end of the jetty. I ask what it feels like? If it feels too painful, and if so, whether she wants me to find Liz again? That of course I will, if that's her wish.

She says no.

I nod, even though it's too dark for her to see. And then she asks if Mama is sick? And I think about it, and say she isn't.

'A sickness is a thing you catch, a thing that finds some unlucky people, and that hopefully they get better from. But that's not your mama. Whatever she has, it isn't something foreign that just turned up one day—something separate to her she came down with. It's something that's been inside her a long time. So we can't really be mad at the sadness just like we can't really be mad at her. They're just…one thing.

So she's travelling now—and it's travelling with her. And I hope they learn to travel well together, eventually. Yeah?'

Anja nods, even though it's too dark for me to see it. And we stare out at the ocean. We watch the thin, curved moon hanging over the ocean, watch a final bird head towards its nest.

Eventually Anja falls asleep against my shoulder.

When it gets cold I carry her home.

# PART FOUR

# SOWING

# 22

## Emma, on Land

After that first evening of talking by the fire, and then that first night of having sex with a nice man, and then that first morning of discovering his daughter has a thousand gold coins like this is a totally normal thing, Conor and I eat toast in bed all day.

But first we must take Anja off to go to her school. She did not explain the coin pile, and I did not ask her to because we are new people and treasure is maybe something you take a while to talk about. Anyway, just after I saw all the coins, the toilet flushed and this was Conor awake. Anja slid the coins into a very old bag and pushed it under the porch and went to get dressed in her school uniform. So her papa does not know she is a millionaire. Families work in different ways.

We go to school, three people walking through this very nice town. And Conor and Anja know people—honestly, it seems like every single person—so they say hi a lot. And Conor always introduces me, and when the other people talk to me— just little words—he smiles, and it is a smile that answers all the questions they do not ask, but which are still very loud.

At the school gate, Anja gives Conor a cuddle (gives his legs a cuddle, the way kids do) and he kisses the top of her head. And then for a moment she and I look at each other like: *Are we cuddling now?* But that moment passes and she gives me a wave, and that is the right thing. Then Conor and I turn around and walk back down the long straight road that is like an arrow, past many colourful shops, all nicely faded from the sea (just perfect). And he holds my hand.

∞

The moment we get back in the door, Emma takes off her clothes. Pulls everything off right in the doorway, and I do too. Then we walk back up the stairs and open the curtains so the light pours in, and we fuck on the bed and on the floor where the blanket landed and on a chair that sits in the corner of the room. She sits on top of me and her tits sit in front of my eyes, nipples large, her skin olive and warm. She drops her head forward, so her long hair falls down over her face and onto my chest, a waterfall of hair.

I let go of her hips and part her hair with my hands and her face is there smiling at me. Emma looks at me, her eyes shining, her neck flushed. She leans forward, puts her forehead against my forehead, and we close our eyes and stay like that, bodies moving, minds still.

I get up and stoke the fire to warm the house and make us toast and have a smoke. And it feels nice doing all these normal things naked. Nakedness gives permission for anything to happen—clothing means there's an order to things, means you're dressed for a certain type of day (a working one or a lazy one or an important one). But when you're naked you might decide to light up a cigarette inside and you do. You might ash it into a cup, just any random one you find. You might hand someone toast and then start having sex again. You might both fall asleep on the floor, no clocks, no plans, the sunlight through the curtains, the dust floating white in the sunlight, her snoring, crumbs on your chest.

∞

We watch a really bad movie and at the end it is the cop's partner who is the killer. And so the cop has to shoot him even though he is his best friend too and even though he also protected a lady in a fight once and was kind of a good man in a way. But also a secret drug-dealer killer guy.

We eat more toast and then I ask who Anja's mama is. And Conor is not awkward about this, but just gets up and walks out of the room and I can hear him rummaging around. And he comes back in with a photo in a frame and hands it to me.

'Liz.'

I could lie but I don't. 'I think I have met her before.'

'That's kind of impossible.'

'Yes, I know.'

And we both leave it like that, with neither of us answering the other's question really. He puts the photo on a table beside him. And then he tips it so she is face down.

And then he says, 'Nup,' and gets up and takes it out of the room and there's more rummaging noises and then he comes back and smiles a sorry smile, and I smile an I-get-it smile, and we fuck again.

And then another sleep and one more toast.

∞

Emma and I get to school pickup early, even though we take our time. Andy walks by and we have a quick chat about his dog. It was having stomach problems, but it's better now. I show Emma things on the way. The apple barges sitting high in the water waiting for the harvest. The church and its stained-glass window—I tell her about the Forest Feast, and she loves that story.

Then I surprise myself and think about something forgotten for a long time. I point up towards the forest, and tell Emma about the nests. How when I was young and inside the home up there on the hill beyond the forest, I used to look down at them. But then when I started working in the book-shop—started feeling happier, lighter—I could start looking up at them. How the staff at the home decided they trusted me enough to let me walk back at the end of my shifts, instead of taking the bus with the other kids. How that walk through the woods and up Prison Hill four days a week made arriving at the gates feel okay. Even made being an orphan feel okay.

I tell her about one group of trees I used to visit, five in a line, one set back. A path I trod into the earth to get there. How I'd reach those five trees and stare up. Fill my lungs with forest air. Stand in the dusk light, in the birdsong. I wonder if I could still find them.

'You want to maybe walk there with me one day? With me and Anja? See if the path I made is still there?' I ask her.

She looks at me like I'm crazy. 'Of course I want to do this.' And she shakes her head and walks on.

Passing the bookshop, I don't say anything, but Emma does. We're walking hand in hand and she stops me, like an anchor stretching my arm back.

'This is a bookshop! On the Main Street! Is this *your* book-shop on the Main Street?'

I nod and feel the quiet pride I always do.

'You were not going to tell me! You were going to keep walking by here.'

'I was going to tell you—just not yet. I'll show you properly another day. When it's open.'

She reads the sign in the window.

'It should be open now. Why are you not in there right now, book man?'

I smile, embarrassed. And she puffs out her chest self-importantly and puts on a voice. 'Oh, it is because of *meeeee*. Very important *meeeee*. Because you had to have sex with me and feed me toast.'

She makes me laugh.

In the schoolyard, we sit on the swings and go back and forth.

'Hey, you remember Andy, the guy on the street.'

'With the grey hair. With the sick dog.'

'He was the last person to see Liz the day she drove out of here.'

'Liz in the photo—Anja's mum?'

I nod.

'Oh, okay.' She does a big push and goes much higher than me. The yard is on a rise and I know she can see the ocean from the top of her arc.

'Your boat still there?' I ask.

'No. It got eaten by a shark in the night.'

'Sorry to hear that.'

'Thank you.'

She slows down again. Slows almost to a stop and looks at me, just the faintest rocking in her. Just the ocean. 'Is it too strange having me be here?'

I go to say no but she keeps going.

'Everything here knows you. Not only the people—all of it. The shops. And the boats. And these swings. They know Anja. They know her mama. I am walking in the middle of it all, walking over her mama. Walking over her and holding your hand.'

'I like you holding my hand.'

'But maybe I am messing up your story. Maybe I will make it angry if we are together.'

I lift myself up on the chains of the swing, holding myself in the air for a bit.

'Why are you smiling, book man?'

My arms sting and I lower myself back down. I look at Emma. 'To be honest, it's just nice to hear it. I've always been the one without a story—no family, no normal place I grew up, no traditions. Everything I have is new. Kid, bookshop, town, friends. Even that sadness with Liz.' I shrug. 'I like having a story. It's even nice to have it worry you.'

I begin swinging sideways, tapping her swing with mine, having her tap me back, a very gentle Newton's cradle.

'But you don't have to be worried. The ones who know our story—like you said, everyone pretty much—they want me to be happy. They want Anja to be happy even more.'

The school bell rings. I get off the swing, offer Emma a hand. 'So make us happy. Let us make you happy. Yeah?'

She doesn't answer, but she gets up and stands beside me.

When Anja comes running out, she points Emma out to her little mate Hannah, tells her something we can't hear.

177

Then she runs over and says, 'We had a blind lady come in with a guide dog!'

When she takes off her bag and holds it out like she does every day, Emma takes it. And Anja lets her, the smallest look exchanged. Then we walk out the school gates and back down the road. When we pass the bookshop, Anja points it out to Emma excitedly. Emma pretends she doesn't already know about it and listens to everything Anja says.

I watch the two of them standing at the window, hands curved above their eyes as they peer in through the glass, and when Anja talks about the dusty smell Emma laughs.

I stand back on the footpath, content, looking at them looking.

∞

After, when Anja is sleeping (she dropped off in the middle of a documentary about polar bears and Conor carried her to bed), I ask, 'Can I phone my papa?'

Conor looks worried. But he does the correct thing and says nothing and just gives me his phone. Which is impossible.

'What is it? Where are the buttons for it?'

He laughs and touches it, and suddenly there are the numbers.

'Wow,' I say. 'Wow that is really…' I shake my head. I push the magically-there buttons and it feels nothing like a tele-phone, but it does still do the job of a telephone and now it is ringing. Probably Papa will not answer it but—

'Hello?'

I cannot speak.

'Hello? Margret? Is the car okay?'

Margret?

'What's happening?' Conor whispers to me, and it is like I am asleep but he wakes me up.

'Papa?' I say into the phone.

'What? Who is this?'

'Papa. Is that you? Are you Gunnar Magnusdottir?'

I hear someone stand up from a chair.

'No. No I am not Gunnar. Gunnar has not had this phone for a long time.'

'Oh, okay then. I…I am Emma. I am Gunnar's daughter.'

I hear him sit down in the chair again. I hear him thinking.

'Emma the Greek?' he asks.

'Not anymore, but I was this. Who are you?'

'Fridrik. Here is Fridrik Einarsson. I had the corner shop in town. I sold you and your brothers chocolate bars.'

'I remember you, Fridrik Einarsson. And I'm sorry to be rude, but why are you in my house?'

'Oh. Oh, Emma,' he says, and that is not a helpful answer.

'Mr Einarsson, is my papa dead?'

And the silence is *yes*.

'Oh. When did Gunnar Magnusdottir die?'

'Emma. Maybe you should be talking with someone else about th—'

'When did my papa die, Fridrik Einarsson?'

He is silent for a long time.

'The next day.'

And now I am the silent one.

'The next day after what? What next day?'

'After you and Ulli. When you drowned. When you and Ulli and your boat did not return and could not be found. Gunnar went then. They found him here. Here in this room. I bought your house, a long time ago now. He was in a chair. By the fire. But the fire was out. His beard was gone. Emma the Greek, where are you?'

I give the telephone back to Conor. All the numbers have disappeared again. This screen is just a black rectangle now.

'What did he say?' Conor asks.

I can hear my breathing in my ears. I can hear Anja snoring gently in the room over us. A log pops in the fireplace and I hear the sparks.

I do not hear the sea. All the waves have stopped.

# 23

## Conor and Emma Forever

We find a shape to our days.

Lying in bed and eating toast is one kind of nice, but embedding Emma into my life, Anja's life, is another. I show her the town, and the woods, and one special day I show her and Anja the birds in their nests—nests I first stared down at from the home on the hill. Nests at the end of a path I thought I'd forgotten, or that would have forgotten me. But it hasn't. The birds have hatched chicks, who hatched chicks who hatched chicks since those first forlorn days. And the nests endure.

Emma starts working at the bookshop. We find a rhythm. I grow a beard and laugh more—a surprised burbling laugh that rises from nowhere and catches me in nice moments. At night, as I wash up before going to join them, I hear Emma and Anja talking by the fire outside, Emma's sentences in their strange shapes, Anja's kid laugh floating on the dunes. And the waves, always, keeping time.

Emma comes to know the town, and to let the town know her. She chats with Alice who makes the coffee. She buys apples from Mr Dahlsen and talks with him about what grows where she's from ('Not much, I think'). She gets her old guitar fixed by a young guy called Ollie who seems very lost but who she sees purpose in. The purpose transfers over to him of course, and he fixes more things and finds out what he needs to do to be happy.

Emma walks Anja to school with me each morning. One evening while planning out the week I shake my head and mutter into my diary that I can't make a parent–teacher meeting, then pause and smile at her across our very old table.

Emma laughs. 'No! I would say terrible wrong things. I would say fuck or shit accidentally and if they say Anja can't read as many words as some other kids, I would say: So what, teacher? She can play the piano and she knows every bird's name.'

But she goes anyway. And she doesn't say fuck or shit. And she comes home deciding she likes the teacher because she said small things which made Anja scratch her cheek with quiet pride. Miss Helen also noted she was a bit shy, and was maybe not putting her hand up for questions when she knew the answers. Anja scratched her cheek in a different way then but nodded that this was true. Miss Helen asked if she could sometimes ask Anja for the answer even if her hand wasn't up—a secret deal only those three in the meeting would know about—and then she could still answer but with less attention on herself. Anja said that sounded okay.

When they come in, Emma flops on the couch.

'Being a parent is more work than trawler nets! And I am not even a real parent. Fuck! Now I can let out all my fucks!'

A burbling laugh rising in me. Anja's shocked gasp, her bright eyes.

The waves outside our window.

∞

Emma grieves. In that first moment of hearing about her dad, her arm stayed frozen when I took the phone from her hand. It hung there, this arm, this hand, those fingers still bent in the shape of the phone. Up till then every movement had felt natural between us, but now I didn't know whether to draw her into me, or lean my weight against her, or give her space, or be perfectly still. In the end I just touched her sleeve and her arm dropped mechanically into her lap. Her eyes stared at a nothing point on the wall. Her mouth moved a bit, nearly said something, didn't.

She rose and walked heavily up the stairs. I followed in silence, just watching. She fell onto the bed and slept where she landed for many hours. The next morning I called Haytham and Maggie and they picked Anja up for school, while I kept watching Emma from the chair in the corner. I read a book (a dog-eared Irish one that throws you around a city), then I slept for a while too, the book splayed on my chest like a tiny blanket.

∞

I wake to her talking to me, most of what she's just said I've missed.

'What?'

'He was not a good papa. He was always busy and always looking at me like I was not his, like I was a puzzle he was trying to figure out. He saved us from the ocean and he fed us from the ocean, but he was not a good papa really—no time for that. Too much work for that.

'So I was waiting. Until I was old enough to meet him as a man, not a papa. The people in our town said he was a good man and I would have liked to know that man. To meet that man, instead of the serious, always-work-to-do one. But now he is dead. Too dead to meet me.'

I put away the book and lie with her. Our bodies know each other again. Her head rests against my chest, my hand smooths her hair, her tears wet my T-shirt. We kiss. We fuck. It doesn't fix anything. It isn't meant to. It's just another thing to do, a next thing to do. Momentum found again.

We grow stiller. Time passes. I think of a story to tell her—a story I read once in a book.

*There's a train. And it passes through every town in the world once a week. And even if your town doesn't have tracks, it comes there too. The train is slow and respectful and it doesn't make a lot of noise like other trains. You can't book it and you can't be late, even if you try to be. It comes to you and not the other way round.*

*The train only takes one kind of passenger—it takes the grieving.*

*Everyone on the train has lost someone, so you don't need to feel awkward when you make eye contact with them. Some might have buried their lover that morning, and some might have lost their mother years ago. But it's not about that kind of time. It's about the time when the grief is at its most raw—the time when you just need the train.*

*Once it has pulled up, you step on and find a seat. And then you stare out the window and the train moves on. It stops at other places after yours, but mostly, you just pass through the countryside and it's dusk and you notice birds sitting on telephone wires and distant clouds and long grass growing beside the tracks.*

*Sometimes someone chooses a seat across from you and you look up and smile, but then you both look out the window again, and it's fine like that.*

*The night comes, and it is long. The train doesn't stop at night—it's a long straight journey without interruption. And that part of the ride can feel lonely, so sometimes people lean in to each other or put a jacket over you if you look cold, but they don't usually talk.*

*During the night they serve food, but you don't feel hungry.*

*After the darkness comes the dawn, and the countryside looks the same as before. You lean your head on the glass and when you pass a town, you notice the washing hanging out in the backyards or the closed curtains of the upstairs bedrooms. You write a word in the condensation on the glass with your finger, and then you rub it out.*

*And a bit after sunrise, the train pulls up and it's your stop. Sometimes there's someone there to greet you, but often not. You step down onto the platform and run your hands through your hair and rub your cheeks. You move your legs a bit because you've been sitting a long time, and you look back at the train. It's pulling out and you make eye contact with someone who's still inside, and wave to them.*

*And as the train pulls away, you lower your hand.*

Her head's still on my chest and I don't know if she's fallen asleep.

Then she says, 'Is this true?'

'No. It was in a book.'

'But is it in a book and true?'

She turns her head and looks up at me looking down at her.

186

'Yes.'

'A grief train will come for me.'

'Yes. Eventually.'

'Okay then. Thank you.'

She turns her head back away from me. A silence settles.

'Emma.'

She doesn't look up. 'Mm?'

'I love you.'

'Thank you for that too then,' she says, and soon she is snoring.

# 24

## Anja

Moratoria.

'It's *moratoria*,' I say, and Mum and Dad nod to themselves.

'Good one,' says Dad and he heads out back to make the tea.

This word puzzle is a small ritual—one we've honed over my sixty years of a life. And like so many small rituals, it fills me with a quiet happiness each repetition.

I go to the player, and flick through the records—Ólöf Arnalds, The Band, Big Thief, Ry Cooder. On and on, fingers running across the sleeves, like walking through long grass. No rush, just waiting for the right one.

Yes. The needle sits in the groove, the button is pressed,

everything turns. Emahoy Tsegué-Maryam Guèbrou plays *Homesickness Pt 2*. Piano keys fall to the ground like rain.

Mum smiles at me and pads across the plush carpet, replaced last year, full and verdant once again. She flips the sign and now we are open. Nothing changes in that moment. We continue doing what we do—shelving, dusting, sorting out the weekend's confusions, translating pen's ink onto a very old computer that will die one day and take every record of every sale with it. We have no backup.

Sitting at the counter, typing away on the clunky keyboard, I look up for a moment. Light pours in through the glass door and it catches the dust Emma has upset. She refuses to use the stepladder and she stretches up, the duster finding the unseen surface of the highest shelf (*Plays*—no one ever asks for plays except their writers, anonymously). She is balancing on tiptoes but she's very stable, very sure. I wish I was that.

Emma cannot give me that, not through her genes. She has tried to teach me, and sometimes it has worked. But I am not of her and so there will always be a different hard-wiring. I have a biological mother's DNA coiled tight inside me like springs—dormant, so dormant, but revealed in funny dangerous moments. Liz's shadow is long and it finds me, rolling over the hills from far away, from wherever she might be.

Emma my mum is brave—she went to sea for years to save someone. And she fought a storm once with a piece of wood. Liz my mother had magic in her too—the things she did were inexplicable. But Emma has a skeleton, a structure that contains all she is. So she can decide when to be extraordinary and when to not.

Liz had no structure, not from my memories of her, not from what Dad or people who knew her have said. Her magic wasn't bad but it also had no rules. She pulsed with it, always wondering if she could hold it in or not, failing to do so more and more. Eventually giving into it and becoming just a blur, like a cloud, like mist. Finally rolling away.

Dad's an anchor. He had to be, because his childhood had no patterns. He was the thing holding his world in place, which is hard and unfair. And later—once he'd found kind people (Maggie, Haytham, others in the town)—he kept being an anchor. But Liz slipped her moorings over and over, and it was a tragedy. Every part of their relationship was. Except me, they both said over and over, smiling earnestly at me across our old wooden table. Never at the same time.

Soon after Liz left, Emma arrived. Just wild enough, but not beholden to the wildness. She knew it in herself—and so she let Dad be the anchor when it was helpful (for her, for him). But she let him be his own boat too. They were two vessels side by side. They've been that for fifty years. Their sea gets calmer and calmer.

'No one's come in!' Dad booms at midday. (He's lying—people have come in, it's been a pretty good morning.) 'Let's close the shop and take the boat out.'

He says that a lot these days. Mum pauses at the highest

point of her stretch, held like that as if it's no effort at all, and thinks. She lowers herself back down onto her heels and nods.

'Yes, okay then.'

Dad emerges from the backroom already holding our three coats, smiling at his mindreading powers, and hands me mine without noticing I haven't answered. We turn off the stereo, turn the sign, turn the lights out.

Ten minutes later we're at the jetty.

∞

We're far out to sea, three fishing lines trailing off the stern. The sea is calm. Mum and Dad and I share a thermos of green tea. Dad and I wear lifejackets, but Mum never will. She lost her mother and two brothers at sea, and all of them were wearing lifejackets when they died. One froze, one was pierced through the heart. One went off, kayaking between the ice floes, a small dark speck visible and then not among the grand white bergs, waving at her daughter on the shore whenever she floated back into sight. Then paddling out of view again. Gone and back and gone and back. And then nothing. Gone. Not vanished into darkness. Into whiteness.

Emma remembers a long time of watching the stark horizon. Looking through squinting eyes at the fierce whiteness, eventually her big and little brother beside her doing the same, then their papa too.

Through his beard, 'Wait here.'

Gruff and to the point.

He paddled quickly, not looking back. Cutting through the glass water, the clouds reflected perfectly upon it. Her papa cutting across the sky. And then him, too, shrinking into the distance, so they worried he might vanish as well. But he did not. He rounded the floe, wasn't there, and then was. Out the other side and looking back over his shoulder, anger etched into him now. Even from back on shore, they felt the heat of it. A quick pivot, the paddle rammed into the water, a fixed point for him to turn on, and then back the other way. Gone behind another iceberg. Returned. His fire growing—but also weakening. They had never seen that flicker of doubt in him before, not even from a distance.

Eventually there was nothing else to do and he was paddling in a straight, defiant line back to the shore. Strong again by the time he'd crossed the sky in the sea once more. Composure returned. A man armed with and armoured by a list of tasks, people to gather, a search party to lead.

So many boats moved back and forth between the clouds that day. Men's voices yelling.

Hope. Then resignation. More searching.

Bonfires on the beach. Not funeral pyres, but not not those either. Women the three children only vaguely knew putting blankets over them, rubbing their shoulders. Ulli didn't take one. Ulli stopped speaking then. The black hole arrived.

All day and into the night, but with the darkness absent at that time of year. No prescribed time to end a search party, no marker for victory or defeat or acceptance. Just light all the time—a drawn out, unending day. Fierce white.

Three children stood on a shore watching frantic adults become tired adults. Hearing the shouts grow less frequent. Noticing people start to avoid their gaze. Giving them food, saying reassuring things. But not looking at them anymore.

Papa cut back and forth. There is no end to his store of energy. His arms do not stop drawing him onwards. People give him space now. They no longer try to ask him questions, or paddle beside him. They don't bring him small cups of alcohol. They don't bring him coffee.

Until eventually everyone is with the children—all standing on the shore beside Emma the Greek and Paddy and Ulli. All squinting. The fierce white. Every head moving back and forth at the same time. Every eye tracking the large man in the kayak paddling hour after hour through the glass. Cutting the sky.

He does not get tired. The night does not come. They do not know what to do.

At last the children are taken home and tucked into their beds.

∞

We get back late from our fishing trip, just as the sun is going down. Emma ties up the boat with the ease of one who fished from it as a child, worked it as a teenager, lived on it, alone, for years. Dad and I head up the beach, either side of an esky full of fish, each leaning outwards against the weight of it, lopsided in symmetry.

At the place in the dunes we turn, through the gate we enter (it creaks and I think to oil it soon, just as I think every day) and under the branches and the birds we walk. Emma catches up with us and presents three knives from the boat. We gut and scale the fish on the weather-beaten table in the garden. It has lived as long as our home. For the first century inside it, then—worn by its years—it was hauled out here. Now we pile fish on it, scrape away their shiny scales, empty out their reeking bellies, and hose the table down once done.

We take the fish inside and Dad puts some in the freezer to smoke later—he has caught Emma's tastebuds.

'You want to stay here tonight?' I offer. 'There's laundry on the spare bed but I can move it.'

But they're okay. They have a glass of wine with me, wave goodbye and then walk home in the moonlight to the little flat above the bookshop, Dad swinging a plastic bag with their night's dinner against his leg.

I sit in my house. It is the size of just one quiet person, with everything in the places one quiet person likes. Between my childhood in the dunes and my middle-aged return to them I spent a small handful of years in other places—a loud impatient city, a very old university campus, in a big house with a wide bed that I shared with a kind woman, in Europe with a man one day younger than me who smoked thin cigarettes on our balcony. But I've ended up here where I began, and a circle feels right. Or something less precise—an ellipse. There's an imperfection to it, a warp. The warp is okay.

I rinse my teacup, fill it with tap water for the night-time, and walk upstairs to bed.

# 25

## Conor in the Morning

I wake up before dawn, and look out the A-frame window at the end of our bed to see snow falling. We don't usually wake up this early. Emma snores a rattling snore—one she's been making a bit lately. I'd better make her a doctor's appointment later.

I rise quietly and slip out of the room naked. We sleep with no pyjamas and lots of blankets as we have for years. Our wardrobe's by the bed and the door creaks, so I go downstairs and find the wash basket instead. I pull out a T-shirt and shirt and jeans and underpants. I find a thick jumper on the back of my reading chair. I find my boots and thick socks inside them. I find a book about the planets lying half-read on the coffee table and, without knowing why, I remove the bookmark.

I creep along the short hall, stepping carefully, avoiding boards that might creak. In the kitchen I ignore the cups on the sink and have a long drink of water from the tap. Most I catch, some runs over my beard and dampens my shirt collar. My beard is white.

I take a jacket from the hook, part the heavy curtain and step into the bookshop. Moonlight floods in through the door's glass, a yellow rectangle that starts on the carpet and bends up the bookshelf. I've read so many of these books. I have not read so many of these books. I walk past them all.

Outside, the darkness is crisp and the door clicks shut. I shuffle my arms into my jacket. I have no beanie or gloves or scarf but I also have no key so I can't go back. I look up at our window and think of something I want to say to Emma, but I can't go back.

I walk up Main Street, not down it, which surprises me. Past the rows of shops, past the suburbs that have expanded out over the seventy years I've known this place. Everyone sleeps. I've known so many of these people. I've not known so many of these people. I pass them all.

I don't look back at the sea. At the blue-black waves, at the white crests, the briny jetty, the house in the dunes, the daughter in the house. I love them all. But I don't look back. I walk towards the woods.

At a point along the road, the houses and shops fall away, yards widen, become scrub, then wilderness. I am in the forest—this time of the morning there are no cars so I walk along the middle of the road. Right here under my feet, the tables of the Forest Feast stood. They say we have one of those tables—we clean our fish on it now.

Beneath my feet is snow. It's fallen lower this year than in a long time and each step I take along the forest road it becomes a shade lighter. It's so gradual I almost don't recognise it, but finally the ground crunches underfoot and I've arrived in a new season.

The road forks—two snow-white paths diverging. But I choose a third. A path remembered. A path I once made. I walk into the woods.

∞

I sit in the bustling church (lots of people all loudly trying to be quiet) and watch Dad's friends file in. They're all there, filling the seats in awkward companionship. Suits mostly cheap and rarely worn, ill-fitting shoulders bumping against each other. Women in dresses nice enough to be formal, but plain enough to be respectful. Kids being told to shush and whispering to each other about there being a body in there, in that box at the front.

Pat, who was in the home with Dad, is there, his wife on one side of him, his son Clinton on the other. Clinton's an invest-ment banker—he's incredibly rich and talks about it often. Pat and Dad laughed about this when they saw each other. But they were always careful not to laugh in front of Clinton. They always stood round whatever new car he had when picking his dad up from one of their long sessions at the pub, making impressed noises and tapping the tyres with their toes.

All the town is here. Some people from the book business are there. Maggie and Haytham would have been here.

Emma seems relaxed. People come up to talk to her, to squeeze her, and she squeezes their hands back, she kisses a cheek or picks fluff off someone's jacket, pats clean their lapels like she's getting them ready for school. I sit quieter of course. All those same people check in with me too, but they know I need a different kind of interaction. They mouth silent words: 'You okay, Anja?'

And I nod small assurances back at them. They give me space.

Emma has a moment of peace finally, all the greetings completed, and she holds my hand, interlacing our fingers, her hand wrinkled, her skin loose. I thank her with my eyes—she leans her head on my shoulder and I lean my head on hers. We are two women, piled on top of each other in a church pew.

The ceremony begins, tears are shed (by me, by Emma, by everyone around us), someone sings a song terribly but lovingly. Father Rourke says some words (but respects Conor's request and keeps god out of it). Light pours in through the huge stained-glass window. The coloured shapes of the Forest Feast—its tables, its cups, its strangers meeting—land upon us all. And then Rourke nods to me. I pick up my neat pages and stand, wade through the silence, climb the three steps. I turn and see the people, lit by stained-glass and old stories, a kaleidoscope of memories. Emma smiles at me and I know I can do this. I read.

*In urban planning it's called a desire line. You find them in public places—where a council has laid a path, but then walkers cut across the grass instead. They choose to shorten their journey, and eventually the grass wears away. Sometimes a clever bureaucrat sees the logic and paves it—they give up plans made and invest in this new one instead. A lovely form of practical democracy.*

*The first desire line I ever saw (and the one I loved the most—the one I think was born of the most love) was made by my father.*

*He grew up in a home for delinquents and orphans that was once an immigration centre, once a hospital, once a prison. It sits on the hill behind us, high enough to get snow. And between our ocean and that home, there's a forest—in which the birds live. And rising out of town (up that hill, over that snow, through that forest) was a desire line.*

*Worn away by his teenaged feet after every shift he worked in a bookshop. Hiking higher and higher, through bracken and native grass, to the place he grew up. Not the walled place that held him. But the wooded place that nurtured him.*

*And standing on a dappled rise, standing among*

*giants, Dad would watch the birds build nests. Or watch them sing. Or watch them teach their young to fly. Coaxing them to a precipice, launching into the air themselves, willing them to follow. An orphan watching families, a prisoner watching freedom, understanding the symbolism.*

*And much later (after the home was closed, after I arrived, after Liz left and Mum sailed into our lives), we'd walk that desire line in the wintertime. Dad would take Emma and me to the end of town, where the line began. And, with jackets pulled to our chins, we'd trudge upwards through the cold, him ahead, us behind. His eyes working hard to make out the path worn in a past chapter of his life—a teenage desire for belonging, worn into the earth.*

*His boots left large impressions in the snow and my small ones fitted inside them, so they looked like ripples, like each footprint of mine was echoing out.*

*Until finally we'd reach the five tall trees, the trees of his youth, and stare up together at the nests. And we'd talk about flying and landing, and the pleasure or sadness of departures, the pleasure or sadness of arrivals. Emma would smile and pour us green tea from an old thermos she always carries. I'd hold my cup with two hands, and watch the steam rise and the leaves drip, and imagine one causing the other. Our breath a mist, our skeletons strong.*

*Once or twice a year we walked that same path, the climate changing, the snow season shortening, my footprints growing bigger. Slowly they filled the impressions left by my dad, until eventually one fit the other perfectly. Until I had taken the lead and he and Mum, older, slower, would follow behind.*

*Until I was the age he was when I was born. The age he lost love. Found love.*

*Until one day it wasn't him who parted the branches or trod this path in the earth anymore. That youthful path of his that led to the nests was maintained not by his footfalls, but my own. The line we now walked was mine. The steps the old couple took behind me weren't purposeful, but simply patient. They were just enjoying joining me for a walk.*

*And I saw it one day, standing in the thinning snow, staring up through the steam of the thermos tea. A bookshop, and a house in the dunes, and the birds and the nests and a line that led to them all.*

*These are my inheritance.*

I fold the pages neatly along their centre crease and make my way back down the three steps. Father Rourke says words of thanks to my thin back, my small shoulders. I accept the thanks with a little smile and walk on. Past the coffin.

Emma pats the pew and I sit down beside her. Her eyes are wet. Her lashes are long and there are tears sitting between them, like dew caught in morning webs. The droplets reflect her eyes—they sparkle, twice. She looks at me intensely. Holds my hand intensely.

'These words you spoke, they were really beautiful.'

Others sitting beside or behind us nod too.

I smile, to her, to all of them, to the coffin.

'Thank you.'

∞

I walk through the woods. The snow is thick and it shrouds every plant it lands on—every fern and branch and burrow. But not the footsteps.

Anja's feet guide me as I walk. In her quiet method there's a great strength. I don't know if I told her that often enough. She is the metronome of our town. Her patient life has taught us all. Except for a short time away, she's spent her sixty years in one spot. When your dad's tumbled into a new place and your mum's run away from an old one, then your rebellion is to return home. And it *was* a rebellion—it used to scare me. Had I not given her the tools, the yearning, for a whole wide world? Had Liz's leaving broken her spirit? Had I not been able to mend it? Had Emma arrived too early? Too late?

But no—Anja is a constant. In a way that seemed very strange once, that seems very right now. Her life is here, in this place. Her feet are here, in this place, and they lead me on.

I reach the trees. I would drink green tea now, but Emma is snoring loudly in a bed in an attic in a town far below me. I hope she does talk to a doctor. I hope nothing's wrong.

I go to a gigantic tree. There are five that are almost a perfect row, but the second one is slightly out of line, a step back. The snow is piled at its feet, sits heavy on its leaves. It has packed itself into small fissures in the bark. I place a hand upon the trunk and walk around it, stepping over great roots, sliding my palm across the scratching contours. I picture myself standing here with Anja, with Emma, our heads raised, a chorus of birds above us. I see us standing side by side a last time.

I climb.

First the trunk offers me nothing, and I have to brace my feet against its neighbour to reach the lowest branch, a massive thing, hugging it with wide arms. Then my feet clamber around until they find a groove, and I jam a boot into it and it gives me the force needed to curl my way clumsily over the top of the limb.

After that first struggle, I get to proper, well-spaced branches that let me reach from one to another: a hand, a hand, a foot, a foot, over and over. I make a lot of progress very quickly (I'm eighty-fucking-five. I haven't climbed a tree for at least twenty years).

And then a new problem, the opposite from the beginning—branches too small. Fearful grabs at whole handfuls of greenery I hope will take my weight. And they do. And I climb. Higher I climb.

I am here now. On top of the world. I sway back and forth with the wind, clinging to nothing at all. The air is thin up here and I savour each breath, clinging to nothing at all. Beneath me is everything.

There is the town, thriving. And the home on the bald hill, crumbling. There is the jetty stretching out to sea—in the water's depths I see the glimmer of imagined treasure and the infinite, looping glide of the drowned.

I see Emma's boat in the harbour. It's not adventuring now, but it might again. Now that I'm climbing this tree, Emma might set sail—who knows?

I see Anja's house nestling in the dunes—Anja is sound asleep. She is sound and asleep. Alone, but not lonely. At peace in a way that gives me peace.

Far beyond the town I see a land of ice and snow. A large man with no beard sits stoically in a chair and takes his last breath. Outside his window an iceberg floats past, a woman and her kayak trapped beneath.

Far beyond the town in another direction is a mansion collapsing in on itself. The humans have forsaken it and dogs—hundreds of dogs—roam the halls of peeling yellow wallpaper.

In a room in that mansion is an old woman—a year younger than me but god she looks old. Liz lies under thin blankets. She writes furiously in a diary.

In a third direction, there's the old sedan rolling over the green hills. Haytham and Maggie are driving home now, and their home is everywhere.

A fourth way. The ashes of a house. Still smouldering, all these years later. Faintest wisps of smoke still rising from the blackened frames. I see shapes of figures, lying inside a room. Two shapes.

And now I see it. The island. Upon it, people smoke cigarettes and watch the clouds and hold their knees and call out in a rage and bury mementoes in the sand and build shelters and toss bottles into the sea and kiss passionately and kiss angrily and kiss gently and write last words and demand things and confess things and laugh and take off their shoes and shave their heads and splash their faces and arrive and arrive and arrive. There are more people than the island can hold, and more keep washing up on its shores, from all sides, with every wave, but it never gets full. It accepts every new citizen and it never gets full. And it never will get full.

And above it all, above forest and mansion and home and jetty and car and town and attic bedroom and charred ruin, they fly. The birds pass in their grand flocks, swooping and cresting, turning as one, diving as one, then lifting again. Riding every current, rounding every peninsula, coasting above each wave. The sound of a million voices exalting. They are a roiling, holy breath. A knot tied and untied over and over. The steam off green tea. A puff of rising earth in a garden. An idea turned in on itself. Her hair fallen over her face. The splash as a chest of coins breaks the surface. As a body does. Cigarette smoke.

I take in the scene, as dark becomes dawn becomes day becomes dusk becomes dark again. And finally, the birds come to rest on every branch, a million billion birds perched around me, shaking out their feathers and their days. And I know it is time. I loosen my grip, loosen my shoulders, set my sights on an island that is calling now. And I tumble.

Tumble until a breath of air finds me, until the current lifts me, until the ground forgets me.

And I soar.

∞

We carry the coffin out into the sunlight.

And we place him in the ground.

# 26

## Emma's Train

It is a half a year since Conor and I went to sleep and only one of us remembered to wake up. Half a year since we buried him. I am lying above the bookshop—just one person in my two-person bed—after a nice day with Anja and her project. It is hard work and so I am very tired. But too tired to sleep. I am sad too—a little heavy sadness reminds me it is there whenever I roll over and discover Conor is still dead.

And then I hear it. I get out of bed and walk downstairs. I put on some clothes but do not worry about a hat or a coat or anything sensible. I walk through the bookshop to the door. But then I stop and go back and pick up a book from the shelf. That surprises me.

I go out the door—and the train is there. A train right here on the street. The front step of our shop is now the platform. There is no rush, from the train or from me. I just pull the shop door shut behind me and climb on. The train goes.

About fifteen people are sitting there. All of them are strangers to me and I think that is the better way. There are lots of seats to choose from, nice padded brown seats and I sit in one all by myself.

We leave town not along the Coast Road or left or right at the Forest Fork. Not bumping along the jetty. Not up Prison Hill. But along all of them together. The apple trees. The fields. My boat tied up. I recognise everything as I pass it.

Then other things I recognise too. My old home in the snow. The place where I shouted at the storm. Even though that is just some spot in the middle of the sea, we are there in that exact spot.

And then the trees. The line of five trees and the nests and the birds. The train fits between the trunks and it stops there for a while and someone brings me green tea and it is steaming. I feel bad for the other people having to wait for me to have a moment in this place, but then I think, hey, maybe they are all seeing different things outside the window. And then I think again, no. No, we're all travelling together. We just notice our things deeper and it makes that bit of time seem longer, just for us.

The train goes on, and I open up the book and read for a while. I haven't read this one before and I don't know if it actually even existed before I reached up and took it. But now it is here and the pages are warm and a bit yellow. I fold it backwards, the left pages behind the right ones so it is like holding just half a book. Like using just half a bed. There is an English word I don't know and he says it to me in a nice whisper like he always does. Always did. And he is not suddenly there being a Conor ghost or anything. He is just being a whisper, that is all.

I finish the book and look out the window. It is night and there's a big moon making a line on the sea, a long shining version of itself stretched forever.

I fall asleep.

I wake up and there is the jetty, the boat, the town, the hill. There are the dunes. Anja, in her garden, sitting on her porch—she is an early riser. She is so strange in lots of ways. I like the ways.

Then the sound of hissing, the grey smoke, the stopping. Outside I see my shop. Our shop. Home. I look and see there are just four of us on the train now. I get off and make it three.

Step right onto the step of the bookshop, my own little platform. Watch the train going away. Wave to it. I look at my empty hand and remember the book is still lying on my seat. That's okay. Maybe someone else can read it. Or maybe it will disappear now. I don't know the rules of ghost trains.

And then I catch myself in this moment.

I feel everything that has built up—since I found him white in the bed beside me, since we put him down in the ground—and I have a big cry, right there on the street. My first one. It is very, very good to feel.

'Thank you,' I say, to Conor or to the train or to whatever, I don't know.

A little thing has changed now.

And changed does not mean healed or ended. Changed just means changed.

I go back inside our bookshop. I climb back up the stairs. Into bed.

Later I will help Anja with her project but right now I am tired. I sleep.

PART FIVE

# REAPING

# 27

## Anja and Liz

The first thing I'll say is how far from the ocean it is.

Liz could have gone anywhere. And who knows, she might have gone anywhere—I have no idea about her in-between years. But now she is here, in a tiny town, on a thankless street, in a forgotten small room which is part of a forgotten old building, so, so far from the ocean.

I pull up my car at the front, step out, and immediately have that niggling whisper of a thought that I should not park it here. It's not a kind thought—it's one full of judgment and cruelty, and I banish it quickly to a corner of my mind I hope never needs unpacking.

The street is silent and the lawn out front of the big house is a mess. About a third is mown leaving clumsy lines of yellowing stubble. And then—at a point of exasperation, perhaps—the mowing has stopped and left the rest shin-high and mangy, weeds and grass competing. The lawnmower lies right where it died. Its housing has been removed and sits beside it, along with a rusted spanner. Who the mower was, what became of them, whether they will ever return—I don't know.

On the front door to the house is a threatening sign about what will happen to trespassers, and also a completely broken door handle. It feels like a caretaker decided it was easier to print the sign than fix the latch. I risk it, and push my way inside.

The 'Hello' I call out echoes in the ghostly stairwell. This building was grand once, but now I wade through its sadness— her note said 3A—to the third floor.

I pass a box that instructs: *In case of emergency, break glass.* And someone did break it. And whatever was inside—held by those two bent clips—is gone. I wonder what the emergency was.

On the third floor, the corridor is so still, the doors so identical, the air so thick that I feel like no one has ever walked here before. My shadow is the first shadow to rise up this fading yellow wallpaper, my foot the first to tread upon this floorboard. Perhaps the microbes in my exhaled breath are the first organisms in this ecosystem—a grand biological evolution will begin from this moment and span a billion years and end with gods and giants.

I hear a wheezing cough, behind the thin wall to my left, and somehow recognise my mother's tired lungs. I could turn and walk back the way I came.

I knock at her door.

I push with a flat fearful palm and the door swings on pained hinges. The room inside is both worse than I imagined, and what I imagined.

'When I run out of dishes, I just get more dishes.' She stands in the bedroom doorway, leaning on the frame and laughing at my expression.

'Your life,' I mutter.

'And no one else's,' she says.

Liz moves slowly and painfully round the room, leaning on things every so often, as if with a sense of what will hold her and what would give way. She opens the fridge and removes a plastic bottle of sparkling water, breaking the seal and pouring it into two glasses that sit pristine by the sink. They are the only two clean things here and I can see they have been waiting for this day.

She returns the bottle to the fridge, even though it contains so little water. Enough that she could have topped up our glasses. Too little for it to ever warrant a future drink, let alone a chilled one. For some reason that decision makes less sense to me than anything else here and I consider arguing, but she looks at me and I understand we are both skirting the edge of a large and dark forest. I step back.

'Thank you.'

She shrugs, takes her glass, walks to the bedroom. Picking up mine, I follow.

Liz sits on the bed and then rotates on her thin bum, back finding an impossible stack of pillows, legs laid out on the blanket. Her knees remain slightly bent and I know she cannot straighten them anymore. She doesn't offer me a seat, and there is no chair, so I stand awkwardly in the doorway holding my water, but not drinking it.

'It's not poison.'

'I know it's not.'

But still I wait for her to drink first. She doesn't, and I feel the forest looming.

'Thanks for coming.'

'Thanks for telling me where to come.'

'But you'd have liked me to let you know a few years sooner.'

'Or not at all.'

It's mean, what I just said, but she smiles at it. I know she speaks this language of gentle violence well, that she has for years—muttering at teenagers in shops, chastising confused tourists—and when I use it too, I see a spark of kinship in her eyes. Those eyes that are still alive, even if every part of the structure around them is crumbling.

'How old are you now?' she asks.

'Sixty.'

'And I haven't seen you since you were nine.'

'Correct.' It's a strange word to use, but I understand my formality.

'You two didn't try to track me down. Didn't come looking for me.'

I say nothing, just take a sip of my poisoned water.

'You didn't have to. Just surprised me that you didn't.'

'We made something new. Emma came into our lives pretty soon after you left.'

'She's very beautiful.' She notices my confusion. 'I saw her at the funeral.'

'Were you there? I didn't know you were there.'

'I know.'

'Where were you sitting?'

Liz smiles. She swivels her finger in the air. 'Around.'

She leans down then, under her bed, lurching her body sideways. Like she's reaching for a weapon. Which she's not, though I feel like anything could be weaponised, by either one of us, in this moment.

She picks up a book and points it at me. 'Bang!' She smiles.

Then she opens the big chaotic volume out on her knees, and papers spill onto the floor.

'Come on then,' she says.

I finish my water, place the empty glass on the floor and walk over to stand beside her, high where she is low, her hair thin, her skull veins. She pores over the book.

'This explains it,' she says.

'What?'

'It. Everything. You came here for answers, so read them.'

'That's not true. I don't really know why I came here.'

'All right, then—I know why for both of us. You have a gap. Your life has a gap. Me—I'm what wasn't there. So here. Fill in the gap.'

'You could just tell me.'

She slams the book shut just as abruptly as she'd opened it and holds it up, staring up at me like our years and roles are reversed. 'This is easier.'

I take the book. It's fragile—I hold it painfully, delicately. The proximity feels funny now and I return to the doorway, half in and half out of this moment.

'If it's just about the scrapbook. Or diary, or whatever this is, you could have just sent it to me. Sent me this instead of your address.'

She nods. 'Yeah, that's true. I don't have an answer for that.'

She lies back on the pillows—they wheeze as she leans her meagre weight into them, tired of her like the whole world is tired of her. I guess she's about to sleep, that the chat's over but I can't go.

'So is that it?' I say. 'You give me a book. And you go to bed. No explanation.'

'The book is the explanation.'

'Your life is obviously ending. It's obvious you're dying. Dad just died, you're facing your own mortality, so you reach out to me. But then—'

'What?'

'You get scared.'

'I'm not scared.'

'You're terrified. Terrified and hiding in bed.'

She roars and it is like an animal's roar. 'I've been more places in this bed than you'll ever know!'

It is the strangest thing to say, full of the strangest anger, answering nothing at all, but at the same time more definite than anything else she might have ever said.

She collapses back. The pillows sigh again. 'Just read the book.'

And my mother gives up on me and simply lies, staring at the ceiling. I follow her gaze—a pack of matches is taped to the ceiling. It makes no sense.

I am left—like I was left the first time, but this time her departure is one of stillness, and it forces me to go.

I set the book down on the floor where I stand, then walk out of the room and through the rubbish of a life. For a moment, I consider dropping a match and simply erasing everything. Letting a fire climb from outcrop to outcrop, across surfaces, over newspapers, fridges melting, glasses exploding, the whole building eating itself.

I don't do this—but maybe only because I'm not sure I would make it out in time.

# 28

## Anja's Project

When I get home from visiting my mother, I tell Emma—
my other mother—everything. So many ghosts and they filled
up her head, and her words were all a tangle, like a jungle
you have to cut your way through with a machete. People are
strange and their minds are strange. I tell Emma this, but of
course she knows.

We sit together in the sad feeling of that visit for a very
long time. And then we turn on the television and we see it
on the news: the fire. A very old building that burned away to
nothing, with one person discovered lying inside it.

I stare at the television. My mouth is a hard line.

'I imagined it—dropping a match, when I was there. And

then she did it. We thought about doing the same thing.'

Emma sees my worry.

'Like we have the same mind.'

'Yes,' nods Emma patiently. 'But, she did do it. And you did not do it. That is the difference, Anja girl. That is why you have different minds. That is why I like yours better.'

And then we sit in a different way, in a warm way, and I decide to tell Emma about the project I've been imagining. And, of course, she loves it.

∞

I dig up the coins. They've sat in a bag, which has sat under the porch for so long—for my lifetime many times over.

I found them when I was young, in that weird limbo of an age and a mood between my mother leaving, and my mum arriving. When Dad and I were feeling both the relief of an end to sadness, and also the weight of the beginning of loneliness. In all other ways, Liz was hard. But in her simply being there, she at least succeeded. And then she wasn't there. And the house felt lighter. But we need gravity—we can't all just be floating.

In that time, I explored a bit, my own timid version of adventure. Dad would often be away in his thoughts, so I'd wander the garden, the dunes, the house. And one day I crawled beneath it. Usually I wouldn't because of spiders, or the possibility of them. But I'd been watching a bird. It wasn't flying that day, just hopping like they do, breaking the soil with quick deliberate pecks, then bouncing to another place and doing the same. Eventually it went under the porch which stood raised on posts at the front of the house.

I got down on my belly and lay my cheek on the cool soil. I stared into the darkness and watched the bird hop through beam after beam of light, consecutive slivers of it that fell between the boards above, one after the other. I watched its feathers, a portion caught in warm rays, another vanished in the darkness. And then I saw a glint, something lying on the earth, in one of those shafts of light, stiller than a bird could ever be. Calling on a bravery I do not possess, I dragged myself beneath the porch.

The bird flew away, of course, and I ventured further into the darkness. The air here was from another time, long undisturbed by humans, cooler than the day, uninhabited.

Fingers in the dirt, pebbles in my forearms, cobwebs in my hair. I reached the coin. It was imperfectly round, ridged and contoured, sure as money. There's a reason coins are made from metal and not stone or wood—those things are hard too, but metal is definitive, intentioned. It feels like human labour.

I went to take the coin, to bring it out into the world. But then I saw another. Coins everywhere. One was stuck to my other palm, several lay one atop another. Some were sticking out of the ground like stalagmites. I was surrounded by a fortune.

I held a coin up to the shaft of light, wiped its grime from it. There was its date, and it was old but not ancient, old enough to impress the child holding it, but not old enough to be a real fortune. Once upon a time, someone must have sent the whole lot rolling, falling down between the slats in the porch, and decided to leave them. Maybe they were very rich. Maybe they just had the amount that pleased them.

I broke the earth open with my fingers to find as many as I could. No delicate bird pecks, just scrabbling nails turning over the sandy soil, finding a coin, setting it aside, finding another, building piles, the piles toppling, lips moving silently, the numbers clicking over in my head.

And then, in the middle of my counting game, I stop. A finger snags something different, musty. Canvas. The corner of an old bag. I ignore the coins now—knock a stack over with my elbow and pay no attention as they slide over each other through the shafts of light. This is a new mystery.

I use two coins as tiny spades, making progress, clearing space. Until enough sand has been shifted to liberate the canvas bag and I drag it out of the earth. It's heavy. So heavy. It takes all of me, and I give all of me, and I free it.

My eyes have adjusted now and I study the old bag in the murky light. No locks or chains—whoever buried this decided the hiding was enough security.

Still lying under the porch, I pull the drawstring, open the top and reach a hand in.

I pull out riches. Treasure. These coins are gold. I hold

history. I hold rarity. And, where one of them alone might inspire awe, I hold hundreds.

And then, among them, a slip of paper. Yellowing, very old. I unfold its crease, feel my brow furrow. A strange cursive, weaving hand, the ink faded but still just there. Seven words.

*For you, Anja. For whenever you are.*

For so many years after I discovered the coins, I did nothing with them. Other than to say I lived above them, and thought about them, and visited them sometimes. As a kid I'd bring a few out into the sunlight every so often, show them to the world, the garden, the waves. Then tuck them back in their bag, back in the earth.

Emma saw them once, so early on in her life with us that it had to be an omen, I was sure of it. I started loving her from that minute, I think, even though I didn't say that word to her for years. Dad never found out about them. I was waiting for the time to tell him—and then fifty years passed, and he grew old, and then he died. And I realised how time works—how you can't explain your rules to time. It is patient, yes, but not swayable.

The day we buried Dad, I dug up the coins. The day after we buried him, I bought the hill.

It's such a strange concept, owning a hill. Of course it's just a piece of land, and pieces of land get bought and sold all the time. But a hill feels different. It towers over us, it watches our lives, it knows temperatures we don't, ecosystems we don't. It feels older—if mountains are history and grains of sand are what they eventually reduce down to, and the space between is aeons, then a hill is definitely closer to a mountain than to sand.

I went online that day of the funeral and found the name of a man in a city. When I arrived at his shabby office, he greeted me (small glasses, bad teeth, folded posture), gave a kindly smile, studied my coins and then studied me in the same way. The man named a price. I thanked him, flew to another city, met another man (who looked surprisingly similar) and I named a figure eight times the first one. He pretended to stew, and I pretended to care, and then he said, 'Yes,' and I became incredibly rich.

I flew home, drove in my old car to a nearby town—bigger than ours, smaller than many—and went to the real-estate office of a man who could sell me the hill. He greeted me (nice suit, not much hair, false eyes) and named a price. I named another one. He pretended to stew, I checked my phone, he said, 'Yes,' and I became much less rich.

I walked out into the sun and took a great expansive breath. I noticed the trees and the cars passing—the people in them, the light reflecting off the mirrors. I noticed the warmth of the afternoon and the pace of the town and the age I'd become and every day that had passed before this one and every hope held for the next. I noticed my body and my weight and my feet on the earth. I noticed the feel of the papers in my hand, the air on my skin, a hunger in my belly.

I got back in my old car, me a sixty-year-old woman who now owned a hill, and I drove to where my mother lived. Where she had lived for years but had only told me in the days after Dad died. I parked outside her house. The lawn was half-mown. I went inside.

# 29

## The Tradition

There is a tradition in our town, an event held on my birthday, which falls late in the spring.

I am not sure quite who started it—it might have even been me. I am old now, my mind is old now, and cause and effect are sometimes tricky to reconcile. The effect is all I seem to notice these days: the things that happen as they are happening. Causes are bigger mysteries for me. I have less time for them.

The tradition happens on Spinster's Hill (formerly Prison Hill). Some people worry this name offends me and they make a point of calling it Anja's Hill but, honestly, I like the name. I think it sounds quite tuneful and it's not a lie, so no use hiding from it. At five o'clock on my birthday, the farmers and shopkeepers and schoolteachers down tools. The fisher folk moor their boats and everyone goes to their homes and puts on nice outfits. The children have neat clothes laid out on their beds for them, and the teenagers select their own. Wives smooth down the fronts of their husbands' shirts with sure, solid sweeps. Then all fill backpacks with bottles and head out, last one pulling the door shut behind them.

Everyone walks up Main Street, backs to the ocean, encountering friends as they go. Most have seen each other recently, so the chats are day-to-day things. But within the crowd are always a few who have returned especially for the occasion—from city jobs or foreign loves or vague roamings—and these ones are greeted with hearty back pats and hugs. And it's nice, soaking up these reunions as we all walk together.

We head into the woods and the light becomes dappled. The air is crisper and the noises are muffled by the canopy, so chat usually dies away and the walk becomes something more solemn—contemplative—as everyone remembers the ritual of the thing they're doing. A lovely, gentle humility descends, the kind that does every soul good. In our hundreds, we walk over the bitumen that covers the dirt where the Founder's Feast was held long ago, here in this very spot. We walk among the tables—the memory of the tables. We walk where our ancestors ate.

And then we reach the Founder's Fork, where the road curls left and the road curls right. But this day is different from every other one, and the dads smile down at their kids and the lovers hold hands and the old (which includes me now) take deep breaths and check their bodies are still capable. And, readied, decided, we head off the road—not left or right but straight ahead into the tangle of the forest.

The first moments are patient ones, as there's just the one gap where every person must step through the thicket to enter the forest. But once that threshold is crossed, that same first step taken by every foot, then the path you choose is your own. It's like when there's a crack in the lintel at the top of a window, and on a wet day the rain drips down at just that spot. But then it does what water does, and begins creeping in its webs down the pane, wending off one way and then the other, trailing straight down for a time but then zigzagging haphazardly. The great unfathomable chaos of water, that one point spawning a hundred arteries which each spawn a hundred more.

Well this is what the humans do on Spinster's Hill, only upwards instead of down. They step onto the base of our hill as echoes of each other—and then they become chaos, and they navigate the trunks of trees, the ferns and streams, left or right or straight or arcing. They circle back on themselves, they skid on bracken and moss, they walk assuredly between hardwood and dead wood and leaning wood.

Some of us—usually the older ones—have our desire lines locked away in our grey heads from the moment we set out. We tread paths we have trod before, and we savour the remembrance of this, of the same steps laid by our younger feet. You carry fewer things when you're old, but you carry more memories. Or more regard for their value.

A mother walks with learned steps in a direction she has long loved. And her son follows behind, proud to learn her path, to slowly—year by year—adopt it as his own. One day he will share this path with his child and so the grand clock will keep ticking.

After a while, the people disperse further and further apart, and it becomes a rare thing to see another person. Particularly if you are slow, as I am these days. I walk at the pace of my ninety years, and soon the woods feel like they belong to me.

And that's true, because they do. Because I planted them.

Three decades ago, when the deed was signed and the hill was mine, I went home and spent a few days planning my next moves. And then I set to work on my project.

My bank account—still far greater than most humans' even after the purchase of the hill—was slowly whittled away, as I made phone calls and sent funds to companies far and wide. And over the months that followed the deliveries arrived. Jimmy, our postman, came to resent me a bit, I think, as his labours grew and his time to park his bike in the orchards and smoke dope with the farmhands shrank. But he never grumbled to me and he made sure each package reached my door with speed and without damage.

Once enough seedlings had arrived, I'd fill my car and drive up through town and turn right at the fork and then turn left at the Prison Road, that winding ominous cut in the bald hill that had serviced armoured vans and delinquent buses and hospital wagons and box-cart cells for two hundred years. Wheezing horses and roaring motors and whispering electrics had carried the damned, the sick, or the forgotten—my mother and father among them—up to that prison, hospital, home. I pictured Dad's detour to the five trees each day, as he returned to that place after working in the bookshop—the branches stretching, the birds and their liberty—before he would trudge the rest of the way up the hill.

Two centuries after the vegetation on the hill was razed so brutally, only a short gnarly weeded grass grew on those slopes, one that could handle the cold menace of the coastal winds. Down low where we lived, the dunes tempered that air—behind the rise, orchards could grow, a town could tick, people could live. Up here though, whatever hoped to exist was chilled and stunted. Stasis. Time forgetting its march. That was the true sentence for those first prisoners, the trauma for those soldiers, the labour for those mothers, the silence for those foreigners, the arrested development for those orphans. Existing in a place that will not let you heal, or age, or birth, or assimilate, or repent. That's why the birds meant something. That's why the town, the bookshop, the freedoms found, unlocked a halted cog.

Momentum. Life is only momentum. But a bald hill does not have it, I realised thirty years ago.

So. I opened up the boot of my car—that first day, and thousands of days after—and I pulled out tools, long handles clumsily wedged diagonally between the back window and the glove box. I lifted out boxes of seedlings and rolls of burlap and stakes. And I set to work.

A million holes I dug over what felt like a million days. A million saplings set down in the earth. A million tripod stakes assembled. A million lengths of burlap cut and wrapped. A million times I drove down a hill. A million times I drove up a hill. Not just for the memory of three parents, but for a million people. A billion.

The past ones and the future ones. The ones who have carried my DNA, or constructed my town, or simply witnessed my life and the lives of others here. The ones I'll never encounter. The ones who sat up here, imagining what could be down there. The ones who would one day walk this hill. Guiding stars. Companions in shipwreck.

And besides our simple, complex human lot, I planted this forest for the ones who would one day nest on this hill and hatch young and fly above it. The ones who would dig burrows. Who would find dens. Swim streams. Hibernate. Hunt. Those ones too.

∞

On my birthday, at the end of spring, everyone walks up Spinster's Hill, treading their own path, led or leading or lost or loyal. My path, of course, is precise and the same every year, and I've known it since young. It arrives at five trees, four in line and one set back. And beneath that one tree, two graves lie. Two headstones, two names. Dad has lain there longer, and Emma arrived later, but their clocks are reset now and they tick together, a steady beat we can't hear. Yet.

I drink green tea from Emma's old thermos, and the steam rises up and my gaze rises with it. I stare at the same branches, the same nests they do, their view now fixed but the world above evolving all the time. An endless cycle of hatch and fly and forage and find and love and breed and hatch that will not end, a great dynastic wheel. I drink tea with Mum and Dad for a bit, say some words that are just for them to hear, and carry on.

Soon I'm high on Spinster's Hill, my hill, and thirty years after my planting project began the forest keeps on being a forest all around me. The canopy is meshed and the ground cover sprawls and the moss climbs and the worms feast and the birds dart. All is alive.

Gradually the incline of the earth beneath my feet becomes friendlier (a relief I feel palpably these days) and suddenly there are people again, friends emerging from the trees in their ones and twos and families. Their cheeks are flushed and their arms swing loose, their breath catching up with itself, their eyes bright. They all look at me, thankful. I look at them, the same. Together we emerge into the great clearing.

And where the building always stood—the prison and hospital and orphanage and every other version of itself—now there is a grand raised floor of weather-seasoned wood, tongue and groove boards atop hundreds of thick posts. A sure, wide ramp ascends from the ground in three zigzags and, like animals stepping onto the Ark, we walk up it. We amble, neighbour shoulder to shoulder with neighbour, chatting about the path through the woods just taken, a new one discovered, an old one remembered, what's grown since last year, what's fallen, the children running between grown-up legs.

Upon the platform sit many long tables and the twice as many long benches. Not handmade like those of the First Forest Feast by my great-grandfather many times over. These ones were brought up the Prison Road (its name unchanged though all else is) on the back of a big truck yesterday, then folded out and covered with tablecloths (thrown into the air with the grand flourish of fishing nets, then left to float down gently and hang low on each side).

The feast itself, though, is like the original. On the earth beside the platform are the coal lines. And above them are the spits, upon which the meat turns. And the sweating cooks of this grand operation—not one man anymore, but a team, led of course by Penny Mulholland, granddaughter many greats over of Niall, Pete, Seb—cut sagely through the flesh and crackle, serious looks on ruddy faces, beer bottles set twisted into the ground by their feet. They pile up meat on long trays, and send these trays off in the hands of teenagers who like the honour of having a job, who know one day they'll be invited to step up to the coals themselves.

And every person takes off their backpack and brings out their plate and knife and fork and spoon and cup and napkin.

And they choose their seats and set their tables. And there are no rules as to where you might set yourself down, but of course there are a million rules as well. And from that same bag or another, everyone pulls out bottles—warm red ones for the adults, fizzy ones for the kids. The brewers proudly lay their longnecks before them, talk reverently of strange alchemies with those who'll listen.

Spinster's Hill hums with a thousand conversations, laughter, corks popping, dishes clacking, benches screeching, a snippet of a song, a child's shout, a baby crying, a person's name called from one table to another, a loving insult, a veiled compliment, a chorus, a mumble, a jubilation. Then, when all have greeted all, I rise.

And I honestly don't know what will happen once I'm dead. I have no idea who will stand at this moment, or if this moment will be done with. I don't know if I should choose a successor. But also, no one chose me. Things happen naturally. If you give a hill back to nature, then a simpler logic prevails. And in a moment like this, humans are a part of that logic, that ecosystem—humans and our funny human rituals.

A hush falls piece by piece—some near me go silent quickly, others are caught in the middle of big loud stories and must be nudged by a neighbour. All eyes turn to me. And my mind turns to the birds.

They sit on every branch around us, visible or not. They sing goodnights or preen their feathers with silent beaks. They are old and slowing, or young and soaring, or tending to their chicks or chicks themselves, or needy hatchlings or embryos imagining the world or cells or the idea of cells. They will, in their lives, soar, changing form over and over and over again.

They will end up on an island, or they will watch us end up there. They will have no opinion about this, or a thousand opinions. They will exist for just a moment, or as long as a bloodline, or as long as a hill. They will be what they did, what they loved, what they missed. What they aspired to. What they destroyed. What they saved. They will be good, or bad, or both, or just a thing existing. Unjudgable. Uncontainable. Chaos. A heartbeat.

I stand beneath them all, every bird there is. And I recognise their faces. And I remember all their names. And I feel my feathers growing. Soon I will climb a tree and fly, I know it now.

But in this moment I stand firm, my footprints echo of all my footprints, at the end of a life, staring out at my friends. They wait. I raise a glass and say, with little fanfare:

> *Thank you for visiting, old friends. I look back over*
> *every day I have shared with you.*

And they nod, as though these words are correct. Then, as the warm wind moves the leaves above, we raise our knives and forks. We share a happy smile.

And we feast.

# 30

## The End
## (And Everything Before It)

From the moment Anja leaves, water begins to pool on the floor. I don't investigate the leak, or call for help. I just watch it happen, watch the tide slowly coming in, over days and days and days.

The water rises, and it carries me up out of bed, the sheet a strange dead thing floating on the surface, me a strange nearly dead thing lying beneath it. I rise slowly higher as the water fills the room.

Finally I open my eyes one morning to find the ceiling just an inch above me. Soon there'll be no more room for me, no more air to breathe. But I'm prepared for the emergency. I reach up and take the matchbox (taped there years before).

I think my last thoughts, and I strike a flame.

I drop the match and see it sink gently down beneath me, through the water, never extinguishing, ready to land on the newspapers and food wrappers. Ready to consume it all. I hold my breath.

The match knows its path. It lands on top of an abandoned book. The moment of ignition is sudden, and then everything is an inferno, an all-embracing roar. The window of my bedroom shatters and every drop of the water that's surrounded me for so long surges out into the sunlight, shards of glass and smashed furniture and me, flowing with it. We pour out of the house as it topples in on itself, ruined in an instant.

I let myself be taken, a rider on the deluge. I'm swept across the half-mown grass, the lawnmower tumbling beside me for a bit, then washing off to other places. I sail down the street of this wholly uninteresting town and the suburbs beyond and the fields beyond that. The water and I surge through valleys, tossed high and low, past farms and alongside a train. I recognise that train, but only from the outside.

Suddenly I'm at the coast, at a huge clifftop, and the water that carries me plummets over the edge towards the water below, the tsunami of my days crashing down on the ocean.

The stream surges and I feel its current pulling me through the ocean far, far out to sea. I fly beneath the surface of the water. Breathing doesn't matter anymore. The coral is bleached and the sharks are hungry and the fish mill in great schools, watching me glide past them.

And then I see it. The island lies waiting for me.

There is its hill but it's new now? Alive and teeming with people I knew, with the nests those people built, a whole town of nests. I know where I am and I see the main street and the bookshop and the house in the dunes. I see the long jetty pointing at me, see the knives and forks and spoons lying on the sand in its shallows, see the infinity shapes curling in its depths.

People are arriving on every shore, just like they always do, always will, forever and ever. And the birds are gliding overhead, watching as new arrivals sit on the sand, cooling their feet in the shallows, struggling to make sense of an ocean just crossed. But this is only a moment, a flash, before they're pulled to the top of the hill and dropped in the place we all begin. The top of the hill is whatever it is for you, and it is always hard, because this voyage is always hard.

It is a place that feels wrong—until a map unfurls, until the birds catch your eye, a town comes into view. That town will welcome you, welcome everyone a different way. You will find your place within it.

For as long as you need to stay human. Until the feathers grow.

The people in the shallows see me travelling through the water and shift politely to make a space for me. And this is not one of the visits I've made here so often, over so long a time. This is different. Now they expect me to stay.

But no. I realise I am not ready.

So.

I tumble myself sideways, fling myself left so fast the current isn't expecting it, and I am in the open water. A person arriving for the first time—which is pretty much all people—won't think to do this, will just let themselves be carried. But grief has shown me the island many times, so I know its ways. I can outsmart it.

I'm old but strong and I paddle furiously, tearing at the waves, putting miles between me and the island. The people in the shallows watch me with worried faces.

I race through the ocean and feel the current dragging at me, trying to haul me back because these are the rules, this is the time. But I will not be taken yet. I've been called stubborn all my life, and I am being stubborn now. I am as powerful and stubborn as a god now, and you do not tell gods when.

I am starting to tire though. The current is strong. It thinks I'm ready for the island and it won't give up. My arms are feeling weaker. The water is feeling colder. There are icebergs in the water. I am swimming in frigid seas. My muscles are seizing up. I begin dropping below the surface. And then fighting my way back to the top. And then dropping again. When I'm below, the current grabs me. Above, I can just about outswim it.

I'm weakening. The cold makes me want to sleep, but if I sleep I know I'll wake up on the island. I fight the current and the stinging in my arms and the cold and the sleep.

I see something red. I see it and drag myself through

the water towards it.

Towards the something red.

I break the surface and I'm there. A kayak. A woman in a kayak. A woman in a kayak beside a great iceberg. It towers over her. She towers over me. She looks down at me.

'Are you okay?' she asks in a language I don't know, but I know what she says. Her face looks kind. She's worried for me. She doesn't understand why I'm here. Arrived out of nowhere. Floundering.

The current sees I'm distracted and it grabs at my ankles. A great surge of force and it's got me. It's pulling me back. So I reach out.

I wrap both arms round the kayak. I hold on tighter than death. I don't plan to—I just do. It's all so quick. Her eyes go wide and she goes to shout but she is tipped. Her face, her torso smashes into the water as the sea pulls at me and I pull at her and she is pulled down with us, with me and the broiling, angry current.

We tear backwards through the water and I know I should let go. But I'm so scared, scared of the island, the full stop of the island, and I can't. I just can't. She's digging at my fingers, trying to prise them off her. But I am strong even though I am old. Her face is turning blue and then white. Her mouth is screaming now but the sea is hushing her. It turns her screams to bubbles and they stream behind her. When they reach the surface only silence is released. Whatever she would have said doesn't matter now.

Her fingers stop clawing at mine. Her screams stop. Her arms stretch out behind her. Like string. She lets herself be pulled along. She doesn't complain. Not like me, fighting and scrabbling. After a while I let the kayak go and roll sideways and watch as the current takes her away, away to the island. Away to the island meant for me.

The water stills. I float for a second, making sense of it all. I bob in the dark ocean, somewhere in its depths. I'm in shock—shock at what I've done. Self-preservation. Something desperate, not planned, not malicious.

But I still did it. I sent her there in my place.

I kick my legs slowly, and rise to the surface. Break the surface. Float upon it, looking up at the birds. None of them can look at me.

She will have reached the island now. I feel terrible. She'll be standing in the shallows now. Little smiles with the people standing beside her. She can take off her lifejacket now, her beanie. It's warm on the island. It's nice.

The stars come out.

The sun rises.

I float on the surface for days and days, wondering what to do, what is right to do.

I decide. I will swim to the island. I will remind the current who I am, confess to it. Go there and stay there, like I'm meant to.

But first, I make a plan. A plan not for me, but for you. For you, Anja. A plan that involves every person you will ever need. I will collect up all the people you will ever need, my girl.

And I will discover if I am one of those people.

I begin.

∞

I am standing on a country road at night. No neighbours here—only on the next hill over. They will race here, but not in time. The house roars, the windows explode, the paint bubbles and melts and runs. The smoke is noxious, even standing back this far. I unzip my black hoodie and tie it round my nose and mouth. I take a big breath, and run forwards.

The porch has collapsed and knocked in the front of the house, which is helpful. I run through the hole in the wall. The living room is an inferno, but the TV is still on. A middle-of-the-night show. A preacher shouting his message. Spare me.

The fumes are so strong but I don't pass out. I drop to my hands and knees, lower than the smoke. Crawl beneath it to a doorway. They're in bed. Engulfed. The bed alight like kindling. Both of them, both at once, no chance.

I crawl backwards out of the room. Turn around. Coughing. Crawl this way. My hands are burning, my knees, the toes of my shoes. A doorway. There he is. Standing up in the cot. Face so red from the heat or from screaming or both. So scared, poor love.

I stand up. Up and into the smoke. Eyes watering. Skin

stinging. Grab him in my arms. Smother him. Hold him. Move quickly. Run before I pass out. Past their bedroom. Through the lounge. The TV has melted. The god man has gone. Out through the hole in the front of the house. Onto the lawn as the house disintegrates behind me. Vomit on the lawn. Put him down on the grass, at the very front of the long country lawn, further than flames can reach. Vomit again. Listen. The sirens are coming, the neighbours. Calm him. Stroke his hair.

It's too late for him.

The smoke is in his little lungs. The rattle, the gasp. But it is not too late for him, not in all ways. I look down at him, stroke his chest with a comforting hand. Tell him about the island. It's so nice. It won't feel that way at first—he'll arrive alone and at first it will be lonely. But then, I will come with a poem. Then a bus ride down a hill. The smell of the books, a key cut, a sunhat forgotten, remembered.

'And then—her.' I'm talking to Conor in a soft voice. A small boy illuminated by firelight. 'She happens. This time the nurses will laugh with relief, will mouth the word *phew*. We'll look at each other and smile. This time that's what will happen. This time she will cry out.'

I tell him all of it. Tell him I'll be there for some of it—but not always. The island is a beautiful place, the town is a beautiful place. I will lie in bed with her, with him, talking about my dreams. But I will struggle. I will have to disappear sometimes, leave the island. I can't live on it like they can.

I tell Conor this, the baby on the grass. He won't remember

it, but I tell him anyway. Tell him of the great happinesses that await him, the man he will grow into there on the island, the father he will get to be. She will sit on his shoulders, will walk in the woods with him, will run out of school and chuck him her bag to carry and talk excitedly about her day.

I promise that to the infant lying on the lawn as sirens wail.

∞

And now give Anja more. Give her everything.

Find the woman on the boat, a moment before the crashing wave, before the one that ends her—don't mention that to her. Instead, alter her geography, map the hour when the tide will draw her in, when she will look out and see the island, see two people on the jetty. Give her to them, them to her. Give Anja that—the love of good people.

*Sail closer to land tonight.*

Emma the Greek agrees.

∞

And now to a garden. I love that garden—it's the thing I miss second-most. I hop from place to place, tap tapping at the dirt. *See me. Follow me.* My girl does. I fly beneath the decking. A glint of something shiny, her small gasp. Her beautiful breath.

∞

Earlier. A war. Be the air. Pick him up. Throw him sideways. The truck turns like a football. Hurl him to the ground. Muddy him. Blood him. The truck lands and all their necks break as one. Blow the dirt over him. Bury him. Lie beside him in the dirt and later whisper to his broken form of a bicycle ride into a small and beautiful town. Tell him to go find its heartbeat. Tell him to build a bookshop. No need to tell him who it's for.

∞

Earlier still. Be a dress. A dress fluttering in a tree. Give her an idea. Whisper it.

*Of course you are meant for children.*

Be the thought that comes to find her often, in her dreams.

∞

Meet her again. Sit with her across a table one day, but not as a bird or a breath of wind. As yourself—with her you can confess. She draws the secrets from people.

Share a pot of tea. Tell her about your girl.

*Is she like you?*

*No. No, she's wonderful.*

You smile and she does too. Good. She understands. Tell her to write a note—when she finds the bag. Give her your seven-word message. Let her deliver it for you.

∞

Earlier. Find him lying asleep on the forest floor. Be the birds that whisper. Whisper of a town. A town he will build. A town that will hold her one day. Be the birds and tell him to bury the coins for later, for her. He will not know her yet, but he will know.

∞

A prison cell. Creep in as he sleeps. Leave a chair. Leave a noose.

∞

Be a dog. Bite down on her shoulder. Stare into her eyes, as the snow falls, as the man puts up yellow wallpaper inside. Silence. Both sit in the silence. Tell the widow to bring coins to the jetty.

The scream of the scullery maid. The footsteps running. Don't let go. Tell her with your eyes.

∞

And last of all.

The house in the dunes. Just before dawn. I creep around the house. My daughter sleeps in a room above. Alone, but not lonely. Seeds are scattered on the table. Trays of saplings in their black containers. All ready for planting. I love her. I love what she is and what she will be. What she is doing. The hill she will make. I do not wake her. She stirs anyway.

When she looks up, I am a bird on the windowsill. Turn my head. Watch her one way and then the other. Watch her watch me back.

I hear the sea, the tide, impatient.

And I know. Okay, no more.

I spread my wings and fly to it.

∞

I'm bobbing. Bobbing back in the water. I put my feet down—already in the shallows. No more running. No more swimming, fighting. Feet down on the seabed, I walk up onto the beach.

At first you're just there. You just watch the sea and the sky and the horizon. Sleep when you want to. Wake up when you're ready. Eat fish you catch. Light a fire. Read a book. Watch the other ones washing up. They all arrive. Everyone does.

Lots of people I know. The woman and her kayak. We wave to each other, warm smiles. No memories. Or no bad memories. You don't need anything you don't need here.

There's the jetty, stretching out to sea now, the children flying off it, not birds yet, but learning, preparing. Treasure in the water—even if it's just forks, spoons, it's all treasure. Everything that washed up is here because someone brought it with them. It's all treasure.

The house in the dunes. I've visited it so often. Lived there so often. Ran away from it so often.

And there's the hill—we all go there first. A piece of wayward glass finds an artery, a truck turns in the air like a football, a house catches fire, a car breaks down in the desert, you are not made for children. We're all too scared to accept the island, so we make the hill whatever it needs to be—to explain itself to us. A mansion, a prison, a hospital, a detention centre, a home for lost youth.

Not Emma though. She was the only one I met who didn't need it. A wave found her boat and then she found the town and its people. Maybe because they called to her, they waved her in, Conor and my girl. Or maybe she did carry death like she always thought. Maybe it carried her too, a knowledge that went both ways. The letter she sent down through the ocean to her mum—maybe that letter got read. Maybe someone told the birds she was coming.

But for the rest of us, it was the building on the hill. Until, eventually, you notice the forest. And then the nests. And then the town. You find its rhythms, find yourself within it, your place. And now I can see it—the island really is beautiful. You just have to exist in it fully, from beginning to end. Until you tumble into the water, or climb a tree to the sky. Sinking or flying.

This island is the in-between. Beautiful.

And now the hill is beautiful too. My girl did that. So even when you start there—scared of what the island is, what it means you've left behind—the hilltop is something softer now. Wrapped in a forest. Welcomed with a feast. With laughter rising and the birds waiting close by. You understand the birds already. You can already picture climbing a tree one day.

I look around. Anja is here on the island somewhere, a child or exactly my age or much older than me and plodding her way up that hill.

Or just a handful of minutes.

∞

It was springtime and the nurses were shouting and people were running (plastic sensible shoes on sterile floors). I'm so weak and my eyes are closing and they're shouting at me, shouting that I can't close them, I'm not allowed to. And Anja—so tiny, so still. They don't shout at her—her they whisper to. Her they plead with. 'Come on, wake up now.'

Then we are going, going away, together.

That was the first time I saw the island. I walked out of the shallows with you in my arms. The tops of the waves gleamed, the birds called. No jetty yet—we were before that. Got to the dunes and I lay you on the sand. Just for a second. Just to take off my hospital gown. Smiling down as you puffed your cheeks full of air, then blew out a sound that made you laugh, made us both laugh. I smiled down at you and…

I am in a house?

A grand house on a bald hill. A tall woman talks at me and my clothes are a uniform and my hands are empty and where is...?

'Do stop being distracted, Betty. I am talking about important things, like wallpaper.'

'Where's Anja? I just put her down and...'

'I feel a headache coming on, Betty, and you are that headache. Focus now. Focus on me now.'

Why is she calling me that? 'My name is Lizzy.'

'Elizabeth, yes I know, stupid girl! And you shorten your long and self-important name one way, and I shorten it another. Fine. You are in my house and so you are Betty. Now, the yellow wallpaper.'

The widow talks on and on. The walls of the stately corridor lean in and in.

Then that same electric snap and I'm lifted again. Good. In a second I'll be back at the dunes. You'll blow a raspberry and I'll laugh at you blowing a raspberry and...

I open my eyes.

Nurses looking down at me. Kind smiles. No. No.

'We thought we lost you.'

I shake my head. Do. Do lose me!

I look around for you, Anja.

Their smiles freeze. Their eyes don't mean to, but instinctively they travel. My eyes follow their eyes. The corner of the room. The bassinet.

You are there.

You are not there.

I pull the blanket to me then. I wrap it round my shoulders, and I never take it off.

∞

I visited the island. I went back, often, all the time. I followed my own footprints over the sand to you. You were always there, waiting in the dunes for me, smiling. No sadness—you don't need anything you don't need here.

So I made you a life, a life in the dunes. From the start of it, to the end of it. I gathered the people and whispered the instructions and visited often to watch it take shape. A township to know you, a bookshop to hold you, a kind man to father you, a kind woman to mother you. That's a hard one, my place being filled like that, I won't lie.

And then coins for you to discover, and a project to inspire you. And time—the time of trees. The time it takes for a forest to grow, for you to grow old watching it grow. I laid out those years for you, Anja, let you fill them as you wanted, as only you could. We all are everything, and you are you. I love that.

∞

And now it's my turn. I am here, bobbing in the shallows. Properly now. Forever now. No more ebb and flow, no more one foot in each world. All here now. I like that, the simplicity of that, the logic. This life. I will like this life very much.

So.

I go back, to a point before. A point I like the look of.

He is planting out a garden when I come. He leans on a spade and watches me.

'It is you. Who I handed matches to once upon a time.'

A nod and a smile. 'I lit one of the candles on your long tables, yes.'

And the wall disappears, and we fall onto a floor, and into a love, and then a garden, and children (who make children who make children who make children, who make her) and treasure and pattern and patience and seasons and the sea, and beginning to end.

Ending on a bench, two old people, sitting on a jetty, sitting side by side. Watching the birds.

See them sail. Tilting left and right into the breeze.

Watch them go.

# Acknowledgments

Thanks first and foremost to the team at Text Publishing—it's a magical thing to have a first novel published, and I will never forget your collective wisdom and generosity. Thanks to Maddy, Fruzsi, Jess, Maddie, Kate, Julia, Ari and Lydia for helping share this story with the world, and to Chong for the beautiful cover.

Most of all, thanks to Jane, for first noticing three chapters in a teetering submission pile and championing them as you did—for a sure editorial hand and wonderful patient way, as you invited me to say more with less, and to make this book all that it might be.

To Essie and Laura, the first to read this tale. To Natalie, the first to be this tale—thanks for a performance of Emma the Greek that made her stay with me for many years after.

To Chris, Claire, Jonathan, Lauri, Lian, Maren, Mary Rose and Summa for such generous support letters as I tried to carve out time to write. The funding never came to be, but your words did more than money ever could.

To friends—this story was written as ill health cast a long and ominous shadow over our household. In that most worrying hibernation, a community proved itself there for us in so many ways that will never be forgotten.

To family, in all seasons.

To Essie, for every journey taken and every nest made.

And to Moe—my son, my sun.